END TIMES

It's Not What It Seems To Be

MARIE O'MALLEY

Marie O

END TIMES
It's Not What It Seems To Be
LOST Baggage Series

Marie O'Malley
P.O. Box 3135
Deland, FL 32721
poetwoman@proton.me
ISBN: 979-8-9866616-0-5
Printed in the United States

Graphics by permission of Doris Hernandez, Playa del Carmen, Mexico

First Printing, First Edition, 2018, Avid Readers Publishing Group Edition
First Printing, Second Edition, 2022, Marie O

Contents

Contents ~ v

What People Are Saying...

What people are saying...

"Powerful themes of female empowerment and spiritual awakening are woven into these entertaining, complementary and easy-to-read stories. Marie O'Malley's unique characters... made me laugh deeply but left me thinking about the injustices of our male-centric culture... Lukas and Sofia's story is one of survival and inspiration as separately, yet side-by-side, they take a deeply spiritual journey to discover the truth of what is hidden inside their exterior selves."
Elisabeth Amy-Vogt, Author and Publisher, ChiqueLit Chickadee Press @emaivot

"... funny and sweet, but at the same time very moving and emotional. I laughed at parts and was sad and angry at other parts. It was easy to get caught up in. I am waiting to read more from Marie O'Malley!!!"
Dana Vaughn, Office Manager

"Marie O'Malley brilliantly explores the emotions of the human psyche through turmoil and trying times in two exceptional stories, La Madrugada and End Times. These two tales of self-exploration, strength and courage make the LOST Baggage series a must read..."
Cpl. Chris Charette, USMC

"A page-turner, filled with likeable and relatable characters, Marie O'Malley's LOST Baggage series is not something you can easily put down. It is heart wrenching at times, yet filled with insight, humour and grace. You will be inspired by its heroine's passion for life, courageous spirit and willingness to evolve."
Gloriane Giovanelli, BA, DC
www.drgloriane.com

"Really loved the story, how Marie O'Malley let us into Sofia's world - the highs, lows resilience, strength and beauty of her inner and outer worlds."
Gay Cachuela, Energy Medicine Practitioner

"... thoroughly enjoyed my time reading this and as you'll see from my notes had personal experiences. The best!"
Vicki Yvonne Ayers, Special Education Teacher (retired)

Dedicated with Love
In Truth and Beauty

To my Mother who blessed me with grit and determination
and
To my Father who blessed me with a great sense of humor
and
To Infinite Intelligence who continues to bless me with
All That Is, Was and Will Be

Acknowledgements

Who can write a book and bring it to publication thinking they did it all on their own? This book, in this form, would not be possible - from inspiration to final creation - without a cadre of friends, relatives, beta-readers, writing group compadres, editors, proofreaders and Fernando, my cat. Your unfailing support helped me reach for the stars to make this book shine and bring it to completion. The errors are mine, all mine.

Special thanks to Diane Charette, Chris Charette, Guglielmo Cameretti, Martha Curtis-Garry, Peter Ragnar, Betsy Amy-Vogt, Lindsey Cosimano, Claudia Napoli, Gay Cachuela, Debbie Braddock, Annely Arrak, Lorenza Villava, Doris Hernandez, Pamela Abel, Babs Griswold, Gordon Strom, Paul Navarro Sanchez, Dana Vaughn, Eric Patterson, Jeanette Strack-Zanghi, James Smith and two great writing groups... The Caribbean Scribblers and the Cassadaga Poetry Club.

Introduction

This book, written in the form of a portmanteau, is one of two stories that make up the complete tale of **LOST Baggage**. Classically, a portmanteau is a large traveling bag that opens into two separate yet equal parts. In olden times, it was meant to "port" (that is to carry) a "manteaux" (or mantle, cape or coat) The word derives from the French language and was first used by Lewis Carrol in his classic, **THROUGH THE LOOKING GLASS.**

However, words do not stay static. Meanings move and change over time, going into and out of style. For examples, just peek into the Old Oxford English Dictionary to find words that have traveled from the rarified peaks of pristine, powerful, positive, loved connotations to the bottom of powerless, pejorative abysses totally abandoned by the speaking public. Such is the fate of some words.

Today's most common meaning for "portmanteau" is one that denotes two distinct words fused together to form a third, a bit like the two sides of the original portmanteau forming a suitcase. Some currently popular examples of portmanteaus are Brexit, sheeple, bromance, infomercial, seascape, tofurky, Bollywood, jazzercise, and many, many more.

I am telling you all this because **LOST Baggage** is written in what I am calling a portmanteau style. That is, there are two stories that stem from one lost suitcase to create the whole tale. One, *La Madrugada* (meaning the dark hours before dawn) is told as a very personal, fictional memoir from the point of view of Sofia who lost her suitcase. The other, **End Times,** is written from the point of view of the suitcase, Lukas, who comes to life to engage in his own magical empowering journey reflecting on some of the larger themes currently playing out in society during the early years of the twenty first century.

Each story stands on its own, alone and is connected by loss, loss of the suitcase. Either can be read first. Such is the magic of this portmanteau. You choose - realism or magical realism - what would you like to read first?

END TIMES

I

LUKAS

Sofia, Sofia! Don't leave. No, no, nooo... Please look at me. You know how lonely I get. Don't abandon me. Please, just glance my way. The guy at the ticket counter had a fight with his girlfriend last night. He is not paying attention to me or anything else. I feel so much emotional pain from him, but he covers it the way polite Italians often do with an outer smile and an inner rock covering his heart. Sleep didn't visit him last night, dark circles under the eyes. Turn around, Sofia... Looooook at me!!!! Pleeeeeease......

Hmmph. She's gone. Didn't even glance this way. It's gonna be cold and lonely when she realizes I am gone, especially when she becomes aware that I have all her new treasures. Angelo! She just kept her eyes on Angelo. Damn Angelo.

Wait... Mmmmm... What smells so good? Oh look, it's Sorelli's Pizza. A couple of years ago, when we were in New York, we ate there, and again, on Lungomare right before the America's Cup Sailboat races. Their pizza is delicious with the light crispy crust, fresh toppings, high-quality cheese. Now here they are at the Naples airport. I love Italy! Great pizza even at the air-port. Yum. All is not lost... But now I sound like a pizza infomercial. Ugh, it's not easy being me.

Someone sees me! An airline guy is coming my way. He looks really buff in that color green. These Italians have style. Just take a look at those shoes. Wow!

Soft glove leather brown loafers with dark blue perfectly spaced stitching. Gotta be super comfortable too. I hope he realizes my flight to Rome is long gone.

He is moving me. Movement is good. Sofia says this all the time. Move the lymph through the body to cleanse toxins. Keeps you free of cancers. Either move or get a massage. Hmmm... a massage is out of the question right now... I have to get back to Mexico, and all those airport massage places are in the terminal. Here down below near the tarmac with a bunch of suitcases, I am just hanging around waiting for the next flight.

Whew... made it to Rome. Short flight. Life is good. But Sofia is long gone. I will catch up with her. Wow... another buff guy checking me out. Must be the orange stripe across my top. Yeah, I look good, and I know it. Rome the Eternal City... also heard it is the city of love... Or is it sex? Either way, my time here is too short to think about having sex. Next flight to Cancun, I am on board. That cute guy with the tight pants said so. Hmmm... wonder how much time we really have. He is a hunk. Tiny bubbles arise in me when he looks my way. Some kind of chemistry is happening here!

Hey... wait... What is going on? Oh no! What a jerk! The janitor just pushed me to the corner with his mop. Hey! Hey! Sweet Cheeks. Over here, I am over here. What's your problem? Everyone have cotton in your ears? Hey! No capisce niente??

What's the matter? No understand English? Italiano? What's going on now? Oh no! I am being moved and fast. Something is not right. No, no, no, noooooooooooooooooooooo.

THuMP, THuMP, THuMP...

Where am I? Smells like an old closed-up beach house with sheets on the furniture. Ewwwww! Can't see a thing. Is this the catacombs? Nawwww, can't be. I was at the airport in Rome a minute ago. The catacombs are near the Vatican. What is this place? Hoo boy, talk about dark, dank and smelly. I don't even want to breathe. But I got to. I must stay alive and get back to Cancun. I miss Sofia. I love her laugh. She lights up my life. She takes me everywhere. She takes care of me just like a mom would.

BUMP...

"Hey... Who did that?"

SILENCE... DARK MUSTY SILENCE.

BUMP...

"Okay... so what's the game?" Lukas said pumping himself up like an old bullfrog with a low, loud voice to make himself sound large because he could not see a thing.

SILENCE

"What's your name big boy?" asked a sultry commanding female voice from the dark.

"GULP!" Lukas could hear his temple pulse-pounding out an SOS distress signal on the side of his head, dot-dot-dot-dash-dash-dash-dot-dot-dot.

"I asked you a question. Are you deaf? E sordo? What is your name?" boomed the voice in the dark.

"La...la...lu... Lukas," he said as a shiver went up from his wheels to his zippers. "Who, who are you?"

"My name is Anna... Inanna. What are you doing here?"

"I doe...doe...don't know," he stuttered. "I was just on my way to Can... Can... Cancun and someone dropped me down a big hole and well... here I am."

"Oh. Hmmm... What did you say your name was? Lukas?"

"Ye... ye... yes, ma'am."

"Damn!!!!" she boomed.

Lukas shivered then recovered, a little offended, asked, "Hey, what's the matter? You don't like my name?"

"No... it's not that. We have just been having some trouble here. We all agreed to ask the Universe to bring us Luke Skytalker. One of us must have been lazy," she hollered into the dark emphasizing the word LAZY. "Va fan culo!" as she wheeled up on two wheels squinting her eyes in the dark. "And we got you! Lukas. Who could not remember to say Skytalker??" she growled. "Lukas! Damn!! Another one of the golden wishes down the drain."

"What do you mean? Who is Luke Skytalker? And what are Golden wishes?"

"It's a bit of a story, but since you are here and will probably be here for a long, long time, I will start filling you in on what's going on."

"You can save your stories, Anna. Just find me an elevator and send me back upstairs. I need to find a flight to Cancun and get back to Sofia."

"In your dreams, Lukas. Ain't no elevators here. Ain't no going home. You might as well accept you are in it with all of us. I will show you around, introduce you to the gang. We have representatives from many cultures, races, creeds, colors, and genders."

"What are you talking about? I am a suitcase!"

"We all thought that when we got here. You will find out the truth. Hopefully, it won't take you too long. You need to wake up."

"But I am awake."

"Yeah... In your dreams, big boy," said Anna.

Lukas looked around. His eyes adjusting to the dark like a cat, he first noticed a cute peach-colored bag with a bulging lower pocket. Then there was the ultra-modern, sleek black titanium case with a built-in camera pocket on his side. A batik cloth bag imprinted with colorful Indonesian exit stamps stood next to an over-sized red leather majestic suitcase with brass buttons on the seam. Turquoise beads adorned its handle. 108 of them.

"These are the guys." Anna moved to the side and adjusted her top pocket a bit, so her ample cleavage was more readily apparent.

"Hi. How long have you all been here?" asked Lukas trying to be friendly and break the icy silence. The odd collection of suitcases just stared at him.

"Wrong question," boomed the black titanium bag in some sort of clipped Asian accent.

"Pay close attention, and all the right questions will be answered in time. Right now, you are required to learn a few rules. I am Hiromoto, Anna's right hand, her right side of the world. When she is not around, you answer to me. Got it!"

"Ooookaaayyy," said Lukas as he rolled his eyes up to the dark ceiling.

"Peachie is from Amsterdam. Karma is from Nepal, and Wayan is from Bali. Of course, I am from Japan. We four represent everything four. Air, earth, water, and fire, West, North, South, and East, four table legs, four seasons, stability, Daleth, four corners of the earth. We are everything four and unmovable. And yet our strength is our problem. Together we are the immovable object. We are strong. We are perfect. However, entropy has set in, and we cannot move very far from each other. We need the sky element to bring us to five and give us space so that we can move independently and create once again. We have important jobs to do, but we are stuck. Remember, movement is life. Staying still is death."

"But you are all suitcases! We are all suitcases!" cried out Lukas.

"Keep dreaming Lukas! How long will it take you to wake up if you think you are already awake?" asked Hiromoto.

"Okay, boys. Enough, enough." Anna snarled in her low sultry Mae West voice. "It's been a long day. Let's go get something to mangia. I hear Sorelli's has made too many pizzas again. Our lucky day but then again, every day is our lucky day, especially since my sister left," Anna sneered and laughed all at once. "Andiamo. Let's go."

Lukas followed this odd mixture of suitcases who thought they were so much more than he could comprehend. They rolled around in the darkness together with a common purpose he did not understand, so he surrendered and followed them. They seemed to know what to do, and he was sure he didn't.

2

ETRUSCANAIR

"Buongiorno. Etruscanair. How may I help you?"

"Hello, my name is Sofia O'Malley. I am calling because you lost my suitcase on a flight from Naples to Rome, Italy and told me you found it and sent it to me in Cancun, but it has never arrived. Can you help me please?"

"Of course, Madame. Please, will you provide me with the case number."

"Sure, it is FCOA219749."

"Oh yes, Ms. O'Malley. We found your suitcase, sent it to Rome and put it on Etruscan Flight A02492. You should contact the airport in Cancun to retrieve your suitcase."

"Excuse me, what did you say your name was?"

"Rafaele."

"Rafaele, this is the same information I just gave to you. The airport in Cancun knows nothing about my suitcase. They never received it. Etruscan Airlines also said they never handled my suitcase. No one knows anything? Can you check to see if it is still with you there in Rome?"

"Ms. O'Malley, I am at a call center outside of Rome. I am in front

6

of a computer screen. I cannot personally check your luggage. Please be patient and call back tomorrow."

"Ooookaaay."

"Arrivederci."

"Arrivederci."

3

THE UNDERWORLD

"So, exactly who is Luke Skytalker?" asked Lukas

"Who wants to know?" answered Karma.

"Well, I do," said Lukas a little indignant, realizing his question had been answered with a question.

"Who are you, really?" asked Karma.

"What do you mean, Karma? Do you think I am some sort of spy?" Lukas answering the question with two questions back to him.

"No, Lukas. You just don't have that kind of light, not that kind of dark shine. I just want to know if you know who you really are?"

Lukas felt a little dizzy.

Another question! He thought, If I tell him I am a suitcase, he will yell at me again. What does he want from me? I never thought about this and don't know what to say. Really, who am I? I feel a headache coming on.

After a deep breath, like a contestant in a Miss Universe Beauty Pageant, Lukas answered, "I was born in New York City. My name is Lukas S. O'Malley. About ten years ago I moved to Mexico near Cancun with Sofia O'Malley. Dancing hip hop and hanging out at the beach are my favorite hobbies. I have perfected the art of waiting, in a dark closet, when I am not traveling."

"Okay... so this is who you think you are. It is just the surface. Take a deep dive. We need Skytalker, and we got you. We have no time to waste," said Karma.

The air had a heavy feel to it when Karma talked. It was hard to breathe around him. It was like Karma sucked up all the available air. But Lukas persevered.

"Who is Skytalker? Is he any relation to the guy from Star Wars?" asked Lukas.

"Wrong questions, Lukas. That was Skywalker, Luke Skywalker. Stick with what you know. All answers are inside of the questions. Only right answers come from the right questions."

Lukas felt dizzy with all this interrogation. His head now was pounding near the side pockets.

It is dark here, I can't breathe, and I have a friggin' over-sized red leather suitcase named Karma acting like the Grand Inquisitor. Who the hell is he? Pompous ass! Lukas thought.

"I heard that, Lukas. Don't move into tangents," said Karma. "Like I told you, we don't have a lot of time. It is critical for us to figure out how to change four into five. The world depends upon us. At least our world does."

"What? Am I thinking too loud for you, Karma?" asked Lukas exasperated.

"Thoughts are things," chimed in Peachie, a light from a dark corner with his soft, lilting Dutch accent. "We can feel your thoughts. Actually, we can feel everyone's thoughts. They are creative and come to us in geometric shapes. Prickly thoughts sting like porcupine triangles, loving thoughts caress like silky smooth enveloping ovals."

"Really?? What kind of world is this?" asked Lukas.

"Now, that, is your first good question? Keep going," boomed Karma from the dark.

Peachie whirled around Lukas and winked at him.

"Ok. So, what kind of world is this? It is dark. It is damp and musty, it stinks. We eat all the pizza we want because the local restaurant can't manage its production and a bitchy but beautiful turquoise soft leather bag with a sexy voice is undeniably in charge."

Lukas continued, "You are all trying to conjure up some obscure fellow named Luke Skytalker who has absolutely no connection to Star Wars, by the way, to relieve you of some type of energetic constipation caused by perfection. And I am just trying to get to Cancun. You tell me, what kind of world is this?"

Lukas' voice reached a loud rumble and a high pitch at the same time as it bounced off the concrete walls; amplified by the dark mustiness.

"Don't get your panties in a wad," giggled Peachie. "We are all stuck here because the world, our world, your world, all worlds are out of balance. Haven't you heard it said that 'Time is Out of Joint?' Everything is out of joint. No one admits that the cause of all this feeling of being stuck is entropy. Entropy is born of apathy. Mistakenly called perfection, it is extraordinarily tiresome. We are perfectly stuck!" said Peachie.

Peachie continued, "We have created a perfect balance for ourselves. The dynamics of harmony, of perfection are in us. You see, we four represent the immovable object. Put us together, and nothing moves. Anna is the irresistible force. Just look at her. Can't you see how attractive she is? It is all perfect, too perfect."

"Well, yeah. Now that my eyes are used to this place. I can see that Anna is gorgeous. Why doesn't she become the fifth element?" asked Lukas.

"Another good question," smiled Peachie. "Before I answer, I want to tell you a little about Anna."

"Her full name is Inanna Sumer. Her beauty, her resilience, and inner strength form a tremendous power that she wields fearlessly. In the past, her sister ruled the underworld. The reasons are complicated for a modern mind to accept, however, Anna - as she likes to be called - from love, loyalty and a sense of justice for all was the first to come to the underworld of her own free will. She came to liberate her sister and stop all the chaos in the outer world. The only problem was that her sister, having lived almost forever in the underworld knew nothing other than killing, maiming, lying and cheating. She was ruthless and tried to annihilate Anna. Left hanging on a meat hook to die, Anna's situation was tragic and hopeless."

Lukas stared at Peachie not quite sure what to make of this story.

"My God, what kind of sisters are these?" asked Lukas.

Peachie continued, "Anna used powerful magic. An intense explosion of forces created from nothing sent her sister to the ethers, but with it, Anna also broke apart into a billion pieces. As she healed gathering bits and pieces of herself and her momentum, Anna remembered parts of her former power and magic, little by little. She had enough to begin using her voice to summon what she needed to pull herself back together. That is how we got here."

"Anna summoned you? How? But tell me first, how did I get here? The Rome Airport underworld is a mystery to me. I was just trying to get back to Cancun," said Lukas.

"You will become aware of everything, Lukas, in good time. For now, you need to understand the physics of the situation. Anna, needing assistance to leave the underworld began calling forth her equal in power, intelligence, beauty, and compassion. We four arrived simultaneously and figured out how to totally harmonize our energies with her as she read us stories from a book she found in a corner. We identified with the stories and became an immovable object magnetized by Anna, the irresistible force. It's all physics, Lukas. Did you ever take physics in school?" asked Peachie.

"No, Sofia and I were English majors, minored in Spanish."

"Oh, so that is why you live in Mexico?"

"Actually, no. Sofia dreamed of opening a restaurant. I went to Mexico to help her after her divorce. We had a fabulous place called Creme Brulé near Cancun that not only served great desserts but featured homemade pasta and fresh seafood delivered to the back door fresh daily by local fishermen. I helped Sofia with marketing. So, what does physics have to do with why you are all here?"

"Have you ever heard of the classic situation when the immovable object meets the irresistible force?" asked Peachie.

"No, not really," said Lukas.

"It is the epitome of stuckness, mired in perfection. It is the exact problem we have here. The world is screaming for change. Mis-creations are destroying everything. It is all wrong. Every day a combination of random cosmic forces and human error make it worse. But you see, it is the end of Kali Yuga. The end times are upon us. And we are all stuck, no movement. Doomsday is looming like a storm cloud. But the end times will not end if we don't resolve this problem of being stuck. The end times will just go on and on tormenting people for eternity," said Peachie.

"Peachie, you seem like a nice guy. I really like the way you move; your accent is pretty groovy too. And I feel some kind of chemistry with you, so I listen to you and trust most of what you are saying. But it scares me to think about the end times and doomsday. I really just need to get to Cancun. I am not ready for all of this. If I understand right, what you are telling me is that if you are successful and break this perfect deadlock you have with Anna, the four riders will come and destroy the world?"

"We are the four, Lukas," said Peachie.

"What? I thought you were suitcases?" asked Lukas.

"There you go again! Let me try to explain so you can get on the fast track. Back in those ancient days, the guys who had visions had no way of knowing the end times would be centered in the subterranean world of the Rome airport. Airports didn't exist in the first century. A guy named John saw us in his visions but could not imagine what suitcases with wheels and zippers were, so he called us horsemen," said Peachie.

"What? You are the four horsemen of the Apocalypse? Stuck in the basement of the Rome airport? And you want me to help liberate you, so you can finish the end times and destroy the world? This is very bizarre." Lukas shook his head in disbelief.

"It's not what you think. Anna read us a book called Revelations, and each one of us woke up and recognized ourselves in the story. When Wayan finishes his prayers, he will explain it to you in detail. In the meantime, why don't you take a siesta? It has been a long day for you. You have a lot to think about," said Peachie.

Peachie wheeled away and left Lukas alone. It wasn't like Lukas could hear anything specific, but in the darkness, he felt the vibration of the busyness of the airport above. It was a hum. The hum gave him hope. There had to be a way outta here.

Lukas wondered how he could be stuck in the cellar of the Rome Airport with the Four Horsemen of the Apocalypse disguised as suitcases. This was worse than a bad dream. What is more, they were all stuck because together they encountered the perfect vibration of an object that couldn't move because it was attracted to an irresistible force of a lovely turquoise suitcase. The insane part of all of this is they needed his help to get unstuck. How ludicrous! Can life get any more bizarre than this?

Lukas thought, I am just a suitcase! A damn good-looking suitcase. But just a suitcase. What have I done to deserve being in a situation like this?

Peachie whispered from the corner, "You are right, Lukas. You are damn good looking."

Lukas sighed, closed his eyes and cleared his mind.

4

WAYAN EXPLAINS

"Om buh buvaha swaha. Om tat savitur varaneyam. Bargho divasya dimahi. Diyoyo naha. Prechodiat. Om."

The resonant sound of the mantra faded softly into the silence. Wayan opened his eyes to see Lukas staring at him. Wayan's hands, still in prayer position as he bowed slightly and said, "Om suastiastu," a typical Balinese greeting.

Lukas didn't know what to say but had often heard Sofia chant Om when she played her crystal bowl. So, he bowed and let loose a short Om, not chanting but speaking it, quickly. "Om," like he was saying hi.

"So, you are our current mis-creation?"

Wayan wore a cloth turban on his head, full of the colors orange, red, blue and purple. Not a whole turban, mind you, but an unusual piece of cloth, more like a broad headband with a top. Looked hand-painted, no machine-like uniformity.

Lukas laughed. "Mis-creation? Now I am known as a miscreation? Must be progressing. At least, no one is yelling at me because I think I am a suitcase!"

"Hahaha. Actually, you are the perfect answer to my prayers, Lukas. Your suitcase nature is apparent, but it is only superficial. Your eternal nature is quite profound," said Wayan.

"What? Someone here actually values me?" mused Lukas a little sarcastically.

"Sure. I do. Peachie does too. Don't worry about Karma and Hiromoto. They like to be heavy-handed and push their weight around if you know what I mean. It is just the part they signed up to play to keep everything in balance. Don't take it too seriously and definitely not personally," said Wayan.

"I am totally mystified. I was on my way to Cancun - you know, turquoise water, crystalline beaches, sun, palm fronds blowing in the light tropical breezes, margaritas, cabana boys, bikini-clad women playing volleyball on the beach, the smell of coconut oil and all that good stuff when boom! My life changed, and here I am in the basement of the Rome airport with you all contemplating doomsday and the end of the world," said Lukas.

"Happens that way sometimes, Lukas. It's okay if I call you Lukas?" asked Wayan.

"Sure. Why wouldn't it be?" asked Lukas.

"Well, each culture has its rules of decorum how to address each other as we get to know each other. I don't want to offend you."

"Wow, you are really different from the rest, Wayan. Please help me understand what is going on. Can I call you Wayan?"

"Sure, sure. Please get comfortable. I will tell you everything."

"It all began with Anna and her altruistic idea of *"helping"* her sister who really didn't want to be helped. A little co-dependent on Anna's part in my way of looking at the world. But it is what it is. This karmic seed began an intense chapter in life for all of us. And it now includes you. This seed of codependency needed fertile ground and right conditions to flower," explained Wayan.

"Anna who had everything... beauty, riches, great health, wonderful husband named Big Jim and a Barbie dream house castle in Portugal was bored with her easy life. She decided to visit her sister who ruled the underworld. At the time, the underworld was not as nice as it is here now," continued Wayan.

Lukas looked around at the dark cellar full of cobwebs, shadows and musty smells with the incessant hum overhead thinking, *this is nice?*

"In those olden days, there was a lot of screaming, moaning, blood and guts as well as bad smells that overwhelmed the place. Anna cleaned all that up. Nowadays a variety of underworld options are available. You can still opt for the hot, smelly sulfur version or the one where everyone cries all the time or the cold hell where even words freeze as they come out of your mouth. Then there is laughter hell. No one ever stops laughing no matter what they feel. It might sound like fun for a while, but your sides and jaw are in constant pain, and everyone derides you incessantly for no reason at all. Could really be called Ego Hell as well.

"Here, now, we have Suitcase Hell in the bowels of the Rome airport. They say, there has never been a suitcase which has gotten out of here intact. And we all know it. Adds a real doomsday element to this type of hell. We know that our owners all have given up looking for us a long time ago. Makes it hard to keep your spirits up. The pizza helps – a type of carb limbo." explained Wayan.

Wayan stopped for a moment, looked up and closed his eyes. He began murmuring something in a low voice as he moved the beads on his rosary with his left hand. Lukas closed his eyes too and waited. He knew how to tarry, after all, he was still a suitcase with lots of practice waiting around, no matter what they said.

"Where was I? Oh yeah. So, as you know, Anna's sister killed her. The sister was crazy mean. She drank too much rotgut alcohol. Some sisters are like that. Miraculously, Anna came back to life in a magical explosion that blew her sister out of the underworld and left Anna herself alive but in a billion pieces, a billion stuck pieces. Ever since she has been trying everything she can remember from her past life to pull herself back together, that is, to recover her soul. The future of all womankind, mankind too, is a stake." said Wayan.

5

CALL CENTER

"Buongiorno. Etruscanair. How may I help you."

"Hello, my name is Sofia O'Malley. I am calling because you lost my suitcase on a flight from Naples to Rome, Italy and your airlines told me you found it and sent it to Cancun, but it has never arrived. Can you help me please?"

"Of course, Madame. Please, will you provide me with the case number."

"Sure, it is FCOA219749."

"Oh yes, Ms. O'Malley. We found your suitcase, sent it to Rome and put it on Etruscan Flight A02492. You should contact the airport in Cancun to retrieve your suitcase."

"Excuse me, did you even listen to what I said? What did you say your name was?"

"Lorenzo."

"Lorenzo, you just repeated what I told you, but the airport in Cancun knows nothing about my suitcase. They never received it. No one knows anything? Can you call someone who might know something new?"

"Ms. O'Malley, I am at a call center outside of Rome. I will radio the airport as we are not allowed to call them. Please hold."

Lively, Italian on-hold music filled Sofia's ear as she sat on hold for a long time, at least three minutes.

"Ms. O'Malley?"

"Yes?"

"I have radioed the Rome airport and suggest that you call us back tomorrow."

"Lorenzo, I should have never checked this suitcase. I should know better than to check in a suitcase going to Rome. I have had terrible luck over the years with my suitcases at the Rome airport, but it was a carry-on. It was perfect to check it in for the short flight from Naples to Rome, so I could stroll freely with my love in the airport. I couldn't think of anything else, except Angelo. Have you ever been carried away by love, Lorenzo? My fingers are crossed that you will be able to give me some positive news tomorrow."

"Arrivederci, Ms. O'Malley."

"Arrivederci"

6

WAYAN CONTINUES

"We four make up the four elements but a fifth element, sky or what you might call space, is needed to complete the power to bring Anna's soul back and thereby set us all free," continued Wayan.

" I thought it was the truth that set everyone free," said Lukas.

"That, too, Lukas. But in days gone by, people knew about the power of the elements. They respected the elements. They knew that each element was as alive as they were. In fact, everything is made up of the same elements – not just things but people too - just different combinations. Everyone realized this way back when. The knowledge was common," continued Wayan.

Lukas listened intently but continued to wonder what it all had to do with him.

"Modern people are out of touch with this ancient way of looking at the world. People are made up of the same elements as the world around them but can't see it. Mental barriers are created between them and everything else. Meaningful connections are rare. Connections to cell phones and wholly manipulated social media have replaced real relationships with other humans and nature. Fake bonds loaded with the feel of real dominate mind space."

"Remember when industry in the Western world tried to replace butter with margarine many years ago? Margarine's not the real thing, a petroleum byproduct, I am told. It is not good for you at all, but with a lot of marketing and publicity, it was touted to be the answer to many health concerns, especially heart disease. The idea never really caught on in Bali or India. We love our sacred cows and the real milk, butter, and cheese they provide for us. Margarine is more of a western thing," said Wayan.

"I don't like margarine, either, Wayan. Not everyone in the West adopts things just because of marketing," said Lukas.

"For us to break free from here, you are our best bet, Lukas, even if you are not Skytalker," continued Wayan.

"Ok, Wayan. I am not quite sure how I am your best bet. What is this thing Peachie was telling me about that you four are really the Four Horsemen of the Apocalypse?" asked Lukas.

"Oh, that." Wayan looked down at the earth and then raised his eyes heavenward once more before closing them and murmuring some un-intelligible words as he moved more beads around the rosary string. His fingers flew over the string of beads in a very well-practiced rhythm.

"Before we talk about the horsemen, I want to explain a bit about what our options are. You see, Anna had access to two more Golden Wishes with which we could manifest things we need. We figured that if we could add the sky element, we could integrate enough energy to create the space and power to break free from the force of perfection that is holding us in place. The plan was for each of us to pray for Luke Skytalker, which is really the pure space element.

"Ok, I get the history. No need to repeat," said Lukas.

"Each of us primarily embodies one element - earth, air, fire, and water. Anna has a little of each element but has not found enough of her pieces to be whole once again. It is a huge jigsaw puzzle, and she needs a few more pieces. Since everything exists in space, the sky element is what is needed, desperately," explained Wayan.

"Obviously, someone or maybe even everyone in our group was lazy and instead of saying the full name, Skytalker, they used the initial S. We each had to say his name 100,000 times. I used my prayer beads to keep track and even added a few rounds for good luck just in case I was distracted and missed a few. Old habit from young monk days. That is how you arrived. Luke Skytalker, Luke S. Lukas. Get it?" asked Wayan.

"I was summoned by you all calling my name a half a million times? Like a crazy sound magnet?"

Lukas closed his eyes and sighed deeply thinking about the days when he was just a suitcase design on a drawing board. *How could it have gotten to this? Life is indeed strange.*

"Now we have to retrieve enough sky element to break free. You are our wild card as you are not yet integrated into this immovable object/ irresistible force deadlock," reiterated Wayan.

"Ok, Wayan. I get your point. Two questions for you, though, how do I, a lowly suitcase with no knowledge of esoteric things retrieve enough sky element to break you free? Moreover, why would I want to, knowing that you will then destroy the world?" asked Lukas.

Once again, Wayan raised his eyes up and then shut them as his fingers flew around the prayer beads. Under his breath sounds, melodic mumbles slipped from his lips.

7

THE FIRE

"Buongiorno. Etruscanair. How may I help you?"

"Hello, my name is Sofia O'Malley. I am calling because you lost my suitcase on a flight from Naples to Rome, Italy, then your airlines told me you found it and sent it to Cancun, but it has never arrived. Can you help me please?"

"Of course, Madame. Please, will you provide me with the case number."

"Sure, it is FCOA219749."

"Oh yes, Ms. O'Malley. We found your suitcase, sent it to Rome and put it on Etruscan Flight A02492. You should contact the airport in Cancun to retrieve your suitcase."

"Excuse me, what did you say your name was?"

"Letizia."

"Letizia, you just repeated what I told you, but the airport in Cancun knows nothing about my suitcase. They never received it. No one knows anything?"

"Ms. O'Malley, I am at a call center outside of Rome. I can tell you what I see in the report. Nothing more."

"Yes, I understand, Letizia. Do you need some time to read the full report? Last time I called, Lorenzo said he was radioing the Rome airport to check on the status. Do you see anything about that in your records?"

"Oh yes, it is here, but it also said that Lorenzo could not complete the transmission because there was a fire at the airport. Only essential communication could happen on the radios at that time."

"Was there a plane crash?"

"Oh no, Ms. O'Malley. Some farmers were burning their fields near the airport. The fires got out of hand. Flights were re-directed for a couple of hours until the fires were put under control."

"And no one thought to follow up on my lost suitcase? Your airline does not seem to be very serious about customer service."

"Oh Ms. O'Malley, we are so sorry, but it looks like it was too shocking for us to have a fire like this. I do hope you understand."

"Can you radio the airport now, Letizia?"

"It is lunchtime, Ms. O'Malley. I am sure no one will answer the radio now. You know they are governed by union rules at the Rome airport and after all this is Italy and it is lunchtime here."

"Well, do I need to call you back, Letizia? Or will you call them when lunchtime is over?"

"It will be best if you call back, Ms. O'Malley. I will surely be on another call when they come back from lunch. Our call center rules don't allow me to re-open a file once we hang up the call."

Silence

"Ms. O'Malley?"

"Yes?"

"I suggest that you call us back tomorrow at a different time."

"Arrivederci."

"Arrivederci."

8

WHO IS REALLY FREE?

"Lukas, please listen to me carefully. There are a couple of ways of looking at what we horsemen are to accomplish. One focuses on destruction. It is true, the old will be destroyed with us or without us. It is how it is. The seed must be destroyed for the tree to be born," explained Wayan. "It's alchemical."

"We live in an imperfect world. It is a world that is ruled by a conflux of corporations, governments, and bored, wealthy people who like to play power games with the slave populations on this earth. People's attention is placed on lies and fear. Focus is drawn to and fixed upon unfulfilled desires, and modern anxiety is magnified by scaring people with constant shocks and violent surprises. It is nothing new, been going on for a long, long time, eons. What is new is the scale of it all," said Wayan.

"Who is really free? Not many. Intelligent people are calling for change, but they are really just as stuck as we are but don't know it. Techniques to keep people stuck are getting more sophisticated. Soon artificial intelligence will take the reins of control if things happen as they usually do, technology will enfold upon itself. Then the earth will face another mass extinction. The horsemen have the power to destroy one-third of everything but, and remember this, they do not have the mandate. There is an element of free will at play here, even for us horsemen. In the end, that is how all visions are. Nothing, absolutely nothing is written in stone. Every vision is a possibility in the moment of the visioning," continued Wayan.

" Wayan, I have no idea what this has to do with me. I came to Italy for a wedding. I really enjoy my life in Cancun. It is a simple life filled with sunshine, fresh air, the beach, the jungle and lots of happy people on vacation," said Lukas.

"Lukas you will soon realize why you are the perfect one to help us. The difference with our stuckness here in the cellar of the airport and the people of the modern world today is degree. Lots of people are stuck in jobs they hate, relationships that drain them, houses that are too big and credit card debt that keeps them plugging away day after day, year after year. Sure, they take two-week vacations to exotic places like Cancun only to return to fifty weeks of slavery that chews up their life force with worry and distraction. Then they are old enough to retire and downsize. And they find their pension doesn't really support an adequate lifestyle because most of their resources go to pay medical bills with high deductibles before their insurance kicks in, if it does kick in, because the list of pre-existing conditions keeps growing like cancer itself. Their pensions are jokes.

"This is not the life dreamed of when they were young. This is a living hell on earth - the most pervasive type of inferno of them all, the living hell. And yet, it is one of the easiest kinds of hell to escape from once you realize it really is hell and not paradise. And there is the rub. Becoming aware. Realizing," continued Wayan.

" Wow, Wayan. I have never heard the world described like this. Maybe I have lived too many years in the closet in Cancun and didn't realize that things were actually getting so bad," said Lukas.

"As I see it, what we four horsemen are to accomplish is to destroy this old imprisoned way of being to make way for the new. Making way for the true Golden Age promised in many of the prophecies of old. A Golden Age of truth, harmony, love, compassion, wisdom, creativity and fun will be born from our work. But it is an inside job," said Wayan.

"Maybe you are describing Cancun, Wayan? At least this has been my experience of paradise for many, many years," said Lukas.

"The new world sings of possibilities for everyone willing to realize who they are. To live this way is so simple. When people realize just how powerful they are and how simple it is to tap into that power, they will drop the shackles that bind them as fast as if they had buttery fingers," said Wayan.

" You are making me think of coconut butter. I love the smell of coconut," said Lukas.

"Those who are invested in keeping the world as it is will have a more difficult time in days to come. Their lies and manipulations will grow more grandiose. But everything will backfire and begin to strangle them. Their violence will expand, grow more fierce and destructive. Their black magic will become as dark as a new moon midnight deep inside a cave. In the end, however, the blackness of their magic will just come back to them and with a vengeance. Ask Karma, he will tell you how that works," continued Wayan.

"For now, know that the birthing of the Golden Age that will last many, many eons depends upon you, Lukas."

"Me? Hahahahahahaha! Meeee?? I am just a suitcase!" said Lukas.

9

PLUGGING AWAY

"Buongiorno. Etruscanair. How may I help you?"

"Hello, my name is Sofia O'Malley. I am calling because you lost my suitcase on a flight from Naples to Rome. Can you help me please?"

"Of course, Madame. Please, will you provide me with the case number."

"Sure, it is FCOA219749."

"Oh yes, Ms. O'Malley. We found your suitcase, sent it to Rome and put it on Etruscan Flight A02492. You should contact the airport in Cancun to retrieve your suitcase."

"Excuse me, what did you say your name was?"

"Paola."

"Paola, please do me a favor and read the whole report. I will wait."

"Ms. O'Malley, I am at a call center outside of Rome."

"Yes, I know where you are, Paola. I am not sure what color the walls are or the color of your chair or what kind of tile is on the floor, but I do know you are at a call center outside of Rome. Do you need some time to read the full report? Last time I called, Letizia said she would follow up with a call to the Rome airport. Do you see anything about that in your records?" Sofia spoke fast, her words clipped.

"Oh yes, it is here, but it also said that Letizia could not complete the transmission because there was a fire at the airport. Only essential communication could happen on the radios at that time."

"I know about the fire. Some farmer's fields got out of control."

"Oh no, Ms. O'Malley. This was another fire, it was in a terminal building. It was in one of the Lost and Found areas. You know we have three Lost and Found areas in Terminal Three. The area that caught on fire is where some of the suitcases are stored until we match them up with their owners."

"Wow, another fire? Three Lost and Found areas? Sounds like an industry. Are the suitcases ok?" asked Sofia.

"Ms. O'Malley looks like some of the suitcases suffered water damage from the firefighter's valiant attempt to save them all. We are so sorry, but it looks like it was too shocking for us to have a fire like this. Chaos erupted. It felt like the world was ending to us. We have saved many suitcases and moved them to a building in the center of Rome. Some suitcases are still in the airport at Fiumicino. I do hope you understand that I cannot answer all your inquiries at this time."

"Truth is stranger than fiction. I really can't believe you are telling me all of this, Paola. I may have to write a book."

"It is lunchtime, Ms. O'Malley. I am sure no one will answer the radio at the airport now. They are very particular about being interrupted during lunch time. It is Italy after all. Eating and food are crucial to us in our culture. Food doesn't quite have the status of sacred in our society but as you probably know, eating and food are held in high respect in Italy. We talk about it, read about it, watch television shows, sing songs and generally live our lives around mealtimes. You must know this if you have traveled here. I hope you understand."

"Sighhhhh... Paola, what do I do? The more time that passes, I feel it is less likely I will ever see my suitcase again. It is only a carry-on. It should not be so hard to find. It is beautiful – blue with an orange stripe with a tag that says, Lukas."

"It will be best if you call back, Ms. O'Malley."

"Best for who?"

Silence

"Ms. O'Malley?"

"Yes?"

"I suggest that you call us back tomorrow in the morning."

"Please let me speak to your supervisor, Paola."

"Ms. O'Malley, I am the supervisor."

"Arrivederci, Paola."

"Arrivederci."

Damn it, thought Sofia as she hung up the call. *I am getting nowhere. I hate being stuck like this. Hell, I am not going to wait. This is ridiculous. I am calling back now!!!*

"Buongiorno. Etruscanair. How may I help you?"

"Hello, my name is Sofia O'Malley. I am calling because you lost my suitcase on a flight. Can you help me please?"

"Of course, Madame. Please, will you provide me with the case number."

"Sure, it is FCOA219749."

"Oh yes, Ms. O'Malley. We found your suitcase, sent it to Rome and put it on Etruscan Flight A02492. You should contact the airport in Cancun to retrieve your suitcase."

"Excuse me, what did you say your name was?"

"Rafaele."

"Rafaele, I already talked with you a few days ago. Do you remember me? I already have all this information, but the airport in Cancun knows nothing about my suitcase. They never received it. No one knows anything? And now I am making a second round of talking with call center operators! I think I am going to scream!"

"Ms. O'Malley, Please calm down. I can tell you what I see in the report, nothing more, nothing less. But yes, I do remember talking with you. You have not had good fortune yet, I see."

"No Rafaele. No luck, no good fortune, no love, no sex, no suitcase, no nothing. I am so frustrated. I feel like I will never see my suitcase again. I had personal treasures in there, even my best shoes because of the wedding."

"Oh, Ms. O'Malley, I am so sorry. I lost my brown leather shoes with dark blue stitching once. I can imagine how you feel. If we do not find your suitcase within 30 days, we will reimburse you for what you have lost."

Feeling a connection with Rafaele, maybe because it was the second time talking to him, Sofia surrendered to the moment. "Ok, Rafaele. So, what do I have to do to make a claim?"

"Ms. O'Malley, just download the claim form from our website, fill it in and when 30 working days pass, you can make a claim," said Rafaele.

"Rafaele, I have lost my suitcase and everything inside, I lose time calling Etruscanair every day, I lose money making all these long-distance calls to Italy, and I have even lost my long-time lover after I thought we were going to get back together again, I feel like I am losing my mind. How much is all of this loss worth?"

"I can't answer that Ms. O'Malley however, there is an FAQ on our website that will explain everything."

"I need an espresso," sighed Sofia.

"Arrivederci, Ms. O'Malley."

"Arrivederci, Rafaele."

10

WHAT TO DO?

What to do? What to do? What to do? thought Lukas.

Can it be true that the old world is going to be destroyed anyway? If so, why do I have to find a way to liberate the Four Horsemen suitcases? Is there some good reason why? Why not let nature take her course? Is there something more I don't understand?

They said Anna had two golden wishes and they used one to call me in. Why not use the other one? This time with more self-discipline. But why am I getting caught up in their problems? I don't even know if I believe in the End Times. It all seems so dramatic to me, like something the churches made up to keep people in line. And… besides who said the End Times are now? Nobody really knows. I really hate it when others put the responsibility on me for things that are none of my business. They seem to have gotten into a fine mess with their stuckness. Incredible. Hmmm smells like smoke around here. I wonder if Sorelli's has burned the pizzas. We may have to opt for the lasagna. Change is good.

A flight to Cancun is what I need. Sofia is so sad, I can feel it. She must be missing me. Is she crying? My zippers feel like they are getting a little rusty. Oh, poor Sofia.

Hey wait a minute. If I tell Anna and the gang that I will help them, maybe they will use the other golden wish to get me out of here. That way I can locate this Sky dude and bring him back to help them. Then I can skedaddle out of here for Cancun.

But wait... Who is Luke Skytalker? Where does he live? Email address? Facebook? Twitter account? Does he even exist? I might be getting myself in over my head. Hello...?? I am in over my head already. Hoo boy.

If I try, there is a chance I will make it back to Cancun eventually. If I don't, I am just as stuck as they all are. Action is the best idea. Change is life. An opportunity exists, I can feel it. They said no suitcase ever got out of the Rome Airport basement alive. Has one ever tried? What do I have to lose? Daily pizza diet is making me fat. Have to use the expanding zipper. This lifestyle is going nowhere.

I have everything to gain by helping them. The gang seems like good guys. Well, Wayan and Peachie are great. And Anna is alright, bitchy but beautiful. She knows how to wield power. The world is going to hell anyway. Look at all the wars, nuclear threats, greed, fake food, fake news, fake people... Maybe the suitcases are right. They will finish the end times with less destruction than if things continue on their usual downhill slide. It could help usher in the Golden Age much more quickly. And I can get back to Sofia and Cancun.

"Ok... I am going to do it! Find Skytalker and bring him back here," Lukas announced to himself in the dark. He felt his zippers tighten up and shine as he stood a bit straighter, determination providing an added strength in his arsenal of qualities.

II

PREPARATIONS

"Ok, everyone. Let's end this stalemate, get on with finishing up the End Times and get the final pieces of your soul back, Anna," proclaimed Lukas to Anna and guys.

"What? Are you going to do it? Great! What's your plan?" asked Anna.

"Plan? Hmm, haven't thought it all through but I am willing to do whatever it takes so I can get back to Cancun," said Lukas.

"Ok, first things first," said Anna, "Peachie, you said you found an airshaft in the southeast corner of the cellar?" Anna straightened up her slouch and took command of the situation.

"Yes, ma'am. And I think if we all stood on each other's shoulders we could push Lukas up and outta here," said Peachie.

"Good. Next, Lukas, you will have to find a human with a good internet connection. Look for someone who is open-minded. I mean, humans are going to think you are a suitcase."

Finally! Lukas smiled at the thought.

"You are going to have to get them to look for Luke Skytalker. Do you know anything about thought transference?"

"New territory, Ma'am," replied Lukas at attention like a new recruit soldier.

"Ok. We will do a quick class on this. You already know that thoughts are things. You could hear the hum of the vibration upstairs and felt the hope it brought to you. You know that different thoughts can feel different - harsh thoughts are like jagged broken glass edges while harmonious thoughts are silky smooth and comforting. We okay so far Lukas?" asked Anna.

"Yes, Ma'am," said Lukas.

"Ok. When you find the right human to work with, get on his frequency. Do what he does, repeat what he says under your breath, smile when he does. Mimic him. Then as soon as you are in the same frequency test it. Send him a little thought like. Check Facebook now. And see what happens. That should be easy. Everyone likes to check Facebook several times a day. Get him to check Facebook, Twitter, YouTube and find Luke Skytalker. Bring Skytalker to us. Got it?" said Anna.

"Yes, Ma'am!" Lukas clicked his wheels as if he was saluting Anna.

"Ok guys, let's do it. Time is a wasting." Light was beginning to shine in Anna's blue eyes. For the first time since Lukas met her, she appeared somewhat happy.

WHAT JAZZES UP YOUR DAY?

"Buongiorno. Etruscanair. How may I help you."

"Hello, my name is Sofia O'Malley. I am calling because you lost my suitcase. Can you help me please?"

"Of course, Madame. Please, will you provide me with the case number."

"Sure, it is FCOA219749."

"Oh yes, Ms. O'Malley. We found your suitcase, sent it to Rome and put it on Etruscan Flight A02492. You should contact the airport in Cancun to retrieve your suitcase."

"Excuse me, what did you say your name was?"

"Nicola"

"Nicola, have you ever lost your luggage?"

"Uh, no I haven't. I don't get to travel much," said Nicola.

"Ok. I know that you are not even at the airport but at a call center somewhere in Italy, right?"

"Yes, ma'am. I have your entire case here in front of me on the computer."

"Yes, I know, Nicola. It is little like a virtual reality game, isn't it?

What are your rules? Do you get extra pay for getting people off the phone quickly? Or for the number of calls you handle during a day? Or the number of 5-star ratings for how polite you are on a call if people hang around to answer the automated computer attendant? Why do you keep doing this boring work day after day?"

"Ms. O'Malley, I can only tell you what I see in the report. It is against company policy to discuss our pay and motivation structure or personal thoughts with clients."

"Nicola, I can only imagine what your day is like. And I wonder if you ever hear from someone who has found their suitcase? I think not. Who would call you to say thank you, we got our suitcase back. Only a very rare soul would do that. I wonder, what jazzes up your day? What makes you go home at night and say to your significant other, 'Honey, I had a great day today!' What could that be?"

"Ms. O'Malley, I am so sorry for everything you are going through. But if we do not find your suitcase within 30 days, we will reimburse you for what you have lost."

"Gotcha, Nicola. Have a great day!"

"Arrivederci, Señora."

"Arrivederci."

13

PEACHIE

"Lukas?"

"Oh hi, Peachie. Have you finished making preparations with the others?" asked Lukas.

"We are taking a break, and I thought this could be a good time to talk with you," said Peachie.

"Sure, what's up?" asked Lukas.

"Ha, ha... very funny, Lukas. Seriously, I really need to talk to you about something important and private. I don't know how to start, but ever since you arrived, I have had feelings for you. I think about you all the time. I feel myself smiling when I think about you. There is some sort of deep bubbling going on inside of me. Do you know what I mean?" asked Peachie.

Peachie felt Lukas' breath as he moved in almost but not quite touching him. Lukas' aroma was like anchovies. Must have been from the last pizza they shared at lunch. It wasn't a bad smell, more like an earthy, musky smell that made Peachie feel warm and cuddly.

"Peachie, I like you. I feel good talking with you, and I get the impression that you understand me better than anyone else here. Feels good. But I must tell you that I have spent almost my entire life in a closet. After all, you know that I think I am a suitcase. It is only since I have been here with you all that I have even considered that I am something other than a carry-on. Do you know what I mean?" asked Lukas.

"Yeah, Lukas. Same thing with me when I got here. When a new identity dawns and combines with some time alone in the dark, anything can develop. It can give you a chance to reflect deeply to connect with your most essential nature. At least, that is what happened to me," said Peachie.

Peachie continued, "When I got here, I really began to get to know who I was for the first time. And it is nothing like who I thought I was. I feel so much more alive now, so much more willing to take risks." He leaned in closer and touched Lukas' shoulder with his.

Lukas smiled, opening up to Peachie, he said, "Yeah. I am thinking that up until now, I have lived a superficial life, traveling here and there but never really settling down, grounding myself into a reality where I could know myself fully. I was always relating to external objects and making sure I looked good but never connecting inside. When I wasn't traveling, my time was spent in a dark closet waiting for the next trip, but I never thought of reflecting on some of the more profound questions in life or of talking to the other suitcases. I just waited.

Lukas went on, "I didn't know suitcases could talk. I didn't know I could talk. Waiting tended to take up all my mental space and focus. I must say that I have just about perfected the art of waiting. It is an art you know. Like performance art, waiting dissolves the moment waiting is over. Do you know what I mean?".

"I know that art, Lukas. All of us who have identified with being suitcases are always waiting. Waiting for the next trip, waiting to board airplanes, trains, buses, and automobiles, waiting to be picked up at baggage claim. Always waiting for someone or something. This is exactly why it is so interesting to think of oneself as something other than a suitcase. Even the idea of waiting transforms. Waiting transforms into being fully in the moment," said Peachie.

"What do you do when you wait, Peachie?" asked Lukas.

"Wayan gave me a set of prayer beads so I can do mantras while I wait, that seems to help take the emotion out of waiting for me because

I spend a lot of time thinking about sex when I am not saying prayers. How about you?" asked Peachie.

"Me? Hmmm, I think about sex too but that's all I do, think about it. My favorite thing to do is determine which nostril I am breathing out of. It grounds me in the moment. Do you know the dominant nostril changes every couple of hours?" asked Lukas.

"How interesting, Lukas. Can you show me how that works?" asked Peachie. His head touching Lukas' side as he now lay on his back looking up into the darkness next to Lukas.

"It's easy. Just focus on your nostrils and breathe in. Which nostril is activated?"

"Both."

"Come on. Pay closer attention," said Lukas.

Peachie closed his eyes and inhaled. "It's the right nostril. Wow! I never thought that we only breathe through one at a time."

"I know, it is pretty amazing when we begin to observe subtleties in our bodies. A lot is going on all the time. We have to keep moving and yet at the same time find time to be still and observe. One of the fine paradoxes of living well is to include both movement and stillness," said Lukas.

"Lukas, you know this, and you still think you are a suitcase?" asked Peachie with a giggle.

"Ok, ok Peachie. So I know a few things. Doesn't everybody?" asked Lukas.

"Yeah Lukas, we all have pieces of the grand puzzle. But don't sell yourself short. Before I knew I was a horseman or what they were calling horsemen centuries ago, I just rolled around and had a good time. Meeting the other horsemen suitcases here, locking into our combined power propelled me to a new level of self-respect. I really began living well. I felt fulfilled, complete. Just when I was at the peak of feeling all this personal power, along came the attraction to Anna. Her irresistible force held all of us in place. One bizarre paradox, we couldn't move. We rolled around as a group of four, no longer individuals and never too far from Anna," said Peachie.

"What do you mean?" asked Lukas.

"If we are free to go out and destroy the things we need to demolish, there is a chance for a new world to be born. You heard all of this from Wayan. And it is true. For you see, destruction is part of creation. We horsemen are only authorized to destroy one third, but we are not compelled to do so.

"It is nothing to be afraid of. Hindus call the three major energies - creation, maintenance, and destruction - gunas. They are part of life. If the destruction doesn't happen as prophesied, we will all fall into entropy. It is already happening. And if it doesn't stop, then the world will really no longer exist. It's like the world will fall into oblivion out of boredom - no movement - perfection. Remember movement is life. Creation needs the energy of destruction to begin again. Does this make sense?" asked Peachie

"I am beginning to get this idea. Is it something like a courageous caterpillar that needs to go into a death chrysalis before the beautiful butterfly is born?" asked Lukas.

"Something like that. Sometimes life is messy. We really need you to liberate us, Lukas. Please don't be selfish and just run to Cancun when you get up to the airport," pleaded Peachie.

"Well... it did cross my mind," admitted Lukas.

"I know. I could feel your thought."

"This is not going to be easy. After all, the world views me as a suitcase no matter what I think of myself," said Lukas.

"Lukas, how you see yourself is the determining factor in everything. See yourself as happy, and your mind is able to filter out anything that doesn't agree. What you choose as your identity is key to how you live. If you see yourself as a lowly, good for nothing scoundrel, then life will agree with you and provide you with those experiences. If you view yourself as a Divine spark of God, however, life will provide you with the proof of the truth. And when that happens, others can't help but say things like, 'My God, I thought he was a suitcase, but Lukas is really Divine!' Do you get my drift, Lukas?"

"Sounds right, Peachie. I will have to try it on for myself and see if it fits."

"What is it they say? Nothing worthwhile is easy. Besides, the important part is that you know you are not a suitcase even though you look like one. Appearances are often not the truth," said Peachie.

"Hoo boy! This is all quite new to me, Peachie. Feels like I have an uphill climb to get on board this train of thought with you." Lukas sighed.

"Lukas, I will be waiting for you. And maybe, just maybe, you will never have to live in a closet again. Maybe you and I can get even closer than we are now. I feel like we have much more to explore with each other. Don't you? Let's pray that everything works out well," said Peachie.

Lukas reached over and ran his hand along one of Peachie's zippers. Peachie felt a shiver go through him and smiled at Lukas knowing the promise inside the tingles.

Anna and the rest of the boys rolled up to a wall at the far end of the cellar. Karma formed the base on the bottom, up against the cold concrete wall. He locked his wheels. Hiromoto climbed on top and braced himself best he could. Next, Wayan took a running roll from across the room and rolled right up on top of Hiromoto. Hiromoto grabbed Wayan's wheels and locked them into notches in the titanium that seemed ideal for the task at hand. Breathing hard, maintaining their balance, their tiny tower swayed a bit.

"Peachie, get over here now," snapped Anna. "We have no time to waste with chitchat."

Peachie looked up at the suitcase ladder and shook his head. "How am I going to get up on top of Wayan? This doesn't look easy to me."

"Don't worry. Your challenge is to be sure you feel for each suitcase as you slowly climb up. Left, right, left. Got it?" asked Anna.

"Ok. And what about you? How are you going to get up, Anna?" asked Peachie.

"See this little trampoline? Someone had tried to bring on board a plane but was rejected as a carry-on and ended up here somehow. It will give me enough spring to get to you. You just have to be sure you remain stock still, so I can grab hold of you. Lukas can use the trampoline too if he can't make the climb himself."

Peachie took a deep breath, noting it was primarily through his left nostril and climbed stealthily up to his perch. Anna bounced a couple times on the trampoline and seemed to fly to Peachie as he correctly held his place. Anna could almost reach the duct-work herself.

Everyone was in place waiting for Lukas. Lukas rolled to the left, then to the right. He moved back and looked at the giant suitcase ladder from a distance. Right about this moment, a little old mouse came out of his hole. Rapidly, he sized up the situation. A fantastic sight of five suitcases, each different from each other and up against the far wall, one on top of the other.

"Don't do it," the old mouse mumbled.

"What? What did you say?" asked Lukas.

"Don't do it. Anna and her gang are not telling you the whole truth. The world as we know it will really end. Haven't you ever read Revelations in the Bible?" asked the mouse.

"No, I was an English major in college," said Lukas.

"Ah man... this has nothing to do with college majors. We are talking about world-class prophecy here. Even though people disagree on the interpretation, a lot of people the world over talk about the End Times. And no one ever talks about it nicely that I know of."

"Who are you?" asked Lukas.

"Gianni Patmouse. Pleased to make your acquaintance. I don't want to scare you or anything. I have had my share of visions. It all started with some tainted cheese. Better than mushrooms but when the visions started coming true... well... I started paying closer attention."

"What do you mean? What are you talking about?" asked Lukas.

"At first, I used some drugs to put me in an altered state and got some pretty wild hallucinogenic visions. I mean, everything was talking to me, even the light bulbs! But then I heard brain scientist Tom Kenyon talking about how taking drugs won't really get you into reality with a capital R. Drugs will only show you the doorway. So, I learned how to enter the visionary field with guided meditations. Finally, I found the way to enter in the visionary realm by changing the frequency of my brain through the sound techniques Tom teaches. With that, my visions have become spot on."

"What visions are you talking about?" asked Lukas.

"Well... these Four Horsemen for one."

"What about them?"

"Well... it is true, they "think" they are the four envisioned a couple of centuries ago on that Greek island. And yes, it is true that they "need" to do their work for the rest of the prophecy to come true. But what they are not telling you is what their "work" really is. Do you really want that karma on your head without even knowing what you are getting into?" asked Gianni.

"I don't want any karma on my head. I really only want to get back to Cancun!" exclaimed Lukas.

"It is already too late for that now, Lukas. You are in pretty deep. Look at them all standing on each other creating an escape for you. Sure, you can just roll on up and over, find the next flight to Cancun and forget about all of this like a bad dream. Remember, though, they have one Golden Wish left. No one wants to be betrayed," said Gianni.

Lukas sat down, bowed his head and let out a deep sigh.

From the top of the suitcase ladder, Anna called out to him. "Lukas, what the hell are you waiting for? We can't stay here all day. Besides, it is almost time for Sorelli's. It is a perfect time for you to get out into the mix of the airport. Please don't let us down. You gotta do it, not only for me, Peachie, Wayan and the boys but for all mankind, all womankind. If you don't... well, you know... everyone is annihilated. Come on," insisted Anna.

At that moment, Sofia came to Lukas' inner eye. She was crying. So sad. She was so alone. It was too much. Everyday Etruscan Air call center employees said the same thing, every day she could find no love in her life. She was stuck. Each day Mexican mosquitoes bit her, and she had to wear the same shoes. Life was unbearable, hot and sad.

Lukas opened his eyes, turned to Gianni Patmouse and said, "Hasta la vista, Baby. I am on my way to Cancun!"

He rolled back and then up and over the suitcase ladder into the duct gaining enough momentum to cruise for a while till he came to a grate which he easily unhooked and dropped to the floor. A little boy saw him, came over and helped him up onto his wheels. *"You ok?"* the little boy asked with his mind.

Lukas realized quickly that this little boy already knew thought transference. What good luck. Lukas nodded. The blue-eyed boy stared straight ahead. His eyes seemed to shine.

14

BARON

Baron grabbed the handle of the little blue and orange suitcase with a shiny metal tag, Lukas. It rolled quickly and naturally behind him as he followed his family group through the airport. The adults, busy talking, planning, on the phone, connected to the internet, seemed as if they were always in search mode, looking for the next whatever. Sometimes Baron felt like he was treated like a stuffed animal. The adults would come and cuddle with him and whisper sweet things in his ear but hardly ever connect directly. No one ever really looked at him in his eyes. It didn't matter, though. He had his own world and really didn't want to connect with anyone's eyes. He gave up relating a while back. It was better that way.

Baron's father was a prominent man in the world, always working. The family lacked for nothing, and Baron even had a manservant, who was also very busy as he had to attend to other members of the family, especially when traveling. No one even noticed that Baron now had his own suitcase.

Lukas looked around at the other roll-a-boards in the group and suddenly felt a little less than, not full-fledged insecurity but the fleeting uncomfortable feeling that comes when you realize you are definitely underdressed for a formal event. Sure, he was a good-looking suitcase, but no gold monograms or fancy leather handles adorned him. A simple, albeit beautifully designed, suitcase who now had to open the extra zippers because of all the recent pizzas, Lukas took a moment to appreciate himself and forget about comparisons. The other bags, while elegant, seemed to have vacant stares like they were hypnotized by something. Even though they were probably full of precious things, they seemed empty, a little like they were flat-lining. The elegant baggage knew without a doubt that they were suitcases, a certainty that Lukas could no longer ascribe to.

Lukas wondered if the little boy would be a useful ally in finding Luke Skytalker. He appeared a little reserved and hadn't yet spoken a word. However, his walk was sure. He seemed quite confident, held his head high. Enveloped by a quiet intelligence, he seemed to live and walk in an energetic bubble of light.

Might be the perfect little boy to help me, thought Lukas. *Let's see if I can do the mind transference thing with him again. I'll start with a question.*

Lukas closed his eyes and thought. *How old are you, little boy?*

Lukas waited. Nothing. *Hmmm... Maybe it was only luck that we connected earlier. I will ask again.*

How old are you little boy? asked Lukas with his mind.

"Who wants to know?" came an answer in the form of a question from the invisible silence.

Uh, oh, thought Lukas. *I hope he doesn't act like the gang downstairs.*

It's me, the suitcase, answered Lukas in the silence of thought transference.

"Ha! I knew you could talk!" thought Baron as he stared out the huge terminal window at the airplanes on the tarmac. Three jumbo jets waiting to board their passengers. Baron counted their windows.

Ok, well please tell me how old you are and what's your name.

"Tell me your name first," answered Baron silently.

Ok, my name is Lukas S. O'Malley. Pleased to make your acquaintance.

"I am Baron Von Camerberg. I am eight years old."

Wow, you really know how to communicate in the silence. Full sentences and everything, said Lukas silently.

"I wish everyone did. People all seem so busy looking at their phones, tv, talking, doing everything on the outside while inside is a jumbled hot mess. You're different," said Baron in silence still staring out the window as if nothing was passing in his mind.

Yeah. Know what you mean. The real juice is inside. So many people are afraid to look at themselves from the inside out. Don't know why. Maybe they think they will get lost or are afraid of what they will find? What do you think? asked Lukas.

"Most people are like fish chasing shiny pieces of bait," declared Baron.

Well, now that is a different point of view. Hadn't heard that one before, mused Lukas.

"Stick around. You may hear more. I have been living inside this little body in silence for a few years now, a lot of time to observe. The family cat communicates easily, but these adults just don't get it. Their minds are too noisy to hear anything."

Baron, we may have the basis for a friendship here. Do you have time for a story? I will need your help but first, let me ask you something. Do you know how to use the internet? asked Lukas.

"Ha! Are you nuts? Of course, I do. My parents signed me up for a special Facebook Account when I was two days old. Youngest in the world they said at the time. It was in all the papers and across every social media outlet. Of course, the only thing posted were pictures. To this day, that is all there is, photos and videos."

Oh Baron, this is so great. Didn't know anyone could have a Facebook account so young. You are a miracle. An answer to many prayers.

"My parents know how to pull strings. They often say that anything can happen with a passport, credit card and a pocket full of money," said Baron.

15

IRELAND

So where are we going? Lukas asked Baron in his mind as they were boarding the plane.

"Ireland."

Really? Wow! Ireland is on my bucket list. Sofia has cousins there. She met them on Facebook a couple of years ago. They are actually first cousins once-removed. Why are we going to Ireland?

"Well, you see my family thinks I am sick because I don't talk to them or connect with them very well. They think it is a vaccine the hospital gave me when I was little. I don't react to much of anything even though I hear and see almost everything going on around me and beyond. The adults throw around words like autism, but a definitive diagnosis has never been made. I don't think the adults really want something definitive. Something about insurance and pre-existing conditions that can follow a person for a lifetime," said Baron in silence.

Autism is something I don't really know much about. Always thought that autistic kids were geniuses but wanted to be left alone, said Lukas.

"Yeah, that is about right, Lukas. It is hard to step down my frequency to communicate with the adults. Besides they don't listen very well and like I said earlier, they tend to treat me like a stuffed animal. It wasn't always like that and it is mainly my fault because I don't like to connect with them. Their *energy feels so chaotic to me. It puts me into overload and is too much for my sensitive system. The periphery is not that bad of a place to hang out. The adult world is so uninteresting to me anyway. Sometimes, I do get lonely, though",* said Baron in his mind as he stared straight forward at the seatback and tray table in front of his seat.

Hey, why are we going to Ireland? asked Lukas.

"My Mom has become quite religious since I was born and believes Ireland has places where miracles can happen. One happened there last year at a place that lots of people saw a vision of the Virgin Mary a lot of years ago. Last year, an autistic kid started talking. My mom hopes we can find a "cure". I am not the one who needs curing, though", said Baron.

Wow. Tell you what. Maybe you don't need a miracle, but I sure do. Do you have time to hear my story? asked Lukas.

"We have about three hours before we land in Dublin. Go for it," said Baron.

The stewardess came by and closed the overhead compartment where Lukas was resting. Distance didn't matter with thought transference, so Lukas proceeded to tell Baron all about Luke Skytalker, Anna and the suitcase gang in the Rome airport underworld. Lukas expressed his desire to get back to Cancun to Sofia. He told Baron about his angst of unleashing the Four Horsemen of the Apocalypse into the world but felt like he had to keep his word, especially to Peachie. He justified that it might even be better to have one-third of the world destroyed and not the whole thing.

"You do need a miracle," said Baron silently as he continued to stare straight ahead. The tray table was now down with a plastic cup of water on it on a neat little round indentation on the right-hand side.

Will you help me find the Skytalker dude? asked Lukas.

"Sure. But do you think Skytalker is in Ireland?" asked Baron.

I have no idea where he is. Do you have an IPad? Maybe we can start there.

Baron opened his IPad and began looking at Star Wars Movie sites. He typed in "Luke Skytalker" and found a few sites. One was of a little boy, who always ended his YouTube Videos by saying "Don't forget to smile." Could this be the Skytalker that would unleash the

Four Horsemen of the Apocalypse on the world? Anything is possible. Seemed unlikely though.

There were other YouTube videos with strange music, reenactments of scenes from the Star Wars series and even footage of a dog with a cape called Johnny Skyewalker. It looked like an ad for whiskey from a Scottish lake region.

A book called, Skydancer was some sort of esoteric Buddhist text written by an American guy living in Nepal. Nothing seemed to fit precisely. No Skytalker on the internet that could bring the space element to the suitcases in the cellar of the Rome airport, so the horsemen suitcases could fulfill a 2000-year-old prophecy.

Baron turned his head to the right and looked out the window at the sky. Blue with some puffy white clouds in the distance. He stared for a long time. Solar rays bounced off the wing of the plane. Sitting in the center of the aircraft near the wing suited Baron while his family was all in first class. Nobody bugged him here, and he felt calm. From this seat, he could count all the screws on the wing. Everyone thought they were rivets, but they are really Phillips head screws.

Lukas awoke from a little nap up above in the cozy dark space he shared with other suitcases above the seat. None of them seemed conscious or had any type of personality like the ones he encountered at the Rome airport. *Any luck, Baron?* asked Lukas in his mind.

"*Nothing exactly fits. An idea is forming, but it is not completely baked yet. Will you trust me with this for a little while?*" Baron asked in thought.

Sure, Baron. What do I have to lose? You are my best bet at finding Skytalker and getting back to Cancun. Take all the time you need. Lukas took a deep breath through his right nostril, closed his eyes and settled back into relaxing.

16

CONNECTION

Ow! thought Lukas. *Something is jabbing my side.* He looked around. Nothing. Next to a green duffle bag, no sharp edges Lukas couldn't figure out what was going on. *Owww! Feels like something intense. What is happening here?*

A moment later, all the air was being squeezed out of him. It hurt. He let out a whimper. *What is this? There is nothing here. Why am I having all these strange sensations?*

Just then, a tremendous wave of fear that had nothing to do with his reality came over him. In the overhead compartment of the plane flying to Ireland with Baron sitting below searching his IPad for clues to the whereabouts of Luke Skytalker, there was no apparent danger; nothing to be afraid of. *Where do these feelings come from?*

Lukas then felt a wave of sadness and became afraid. Tears formed in his eyes and the thought of Sofia entered his mind. He really wanted to get back with her. *Why am I so worried? I am now on the right path. I help the suitcases break their stalemate, and I get to go back to Cancun. Soon, Sofia and I will be together again. I can feel it. I don't understand why am I having all these strange feelings? These sensations don't feel like they belong to me.*

How is Sofia doing? thought Lukas. *She loves to go to the beach. I hope she is doing that. Something doesn't feel right. It's the middle of the night in Mexico right now. I hope Sofia is ok.*

17

GREY AND GREEN

Hey Baron, projected Lukas in thought. *Everything really is green here, even the walls of the airport. The Emerald Isle.*

"*Lukas, please look at the sky. What do you see?*" asked Baron in thought.

Well, ok, it is grey with heavy clouds. Makes the green stick out even more, answered Lukas cheerfully.

They walked out of the Dublin Airport together into the waiting white limo. Baron stared straight ahead in the roomy interior which was like a living room. Facing backward in the car, he could see Lukas clearly. They were on the way to Knock.

Baron, something's not right with Sofia. My connection to her is down. I have really lost her. Do you think she died?

Baron closed his eyes and took a long, slow deep breath.

"*Lukas, I can see Sofia in my mind's eye. She is very pretty but was in some deep trouble last night. She survived but is not doing well. She is fragile, crying all the time. I don't know exactly what has happened. Seems as if she was attacked by someone with a knife. A man named Angelo is taking care of her. Do you know him?*" asked Baron.

I knew it. Something is very wrong with Sofia. Why, oh why, am I here in Ireland? I should be in Cancun, said Lukas.

"But what about the Four Horsemen, Luke Skytalker and the fate of the world, Lukas?" asked Baron.

Oh yeah, that. Hmmph. My God, it just doesn't seem that important when someone you love is in trouble. I feel like I am trembling inside. It's urgent that we find Skytalker quickly, so I can get back to Cancun, said Lukas in thought.

The car sped west toward Knock passing by rolling green fields, sheep, cows and beautiful countryside of County Mayo.

"Lukas don't worry. We never know what is around the next corner. If we have good insides, we can get through anything," projected Baron.

Baron closed his eyes again. This time, he fell asleep sitting straight up. It had already been a long day, and not yet noon. Lukas rested but could not hold back tears thinking about Sofia. What had happened to her?

18

KNOCK

Baron's family could have flown into Knock, but the limo ride was so comfortable, and Baron's father had a conference call that lasted three hours, almost the entire trip. Green fields and little hamlets gave them time to realize where we were as drove into western Ireland. Lukas thought about Sofia and prayed that she was ok. When Sofia came to mind, though, he trembled inside. She was still in trouble.

Close to Knock, in Claremorris, the group settled into a beautiful, big hotel with an indoor swimming pool, a boon because it was cold, windy and rainy outside. Heavy grey clouds formed a solid mass over the town.

Many of the people staying at the hotel seemed to have problems. Old and young walking with crutches, walkers, and canes while others rolled around in wheelchairs. Still, others didn't seem to have physical issues but had vacant looks on their faces. Grimaces revealed some sort of inner pain. Then there were those who may have been expert at masking problems. On the outside, they seemed perfectly fine, happy even. But Lukas wondered about them. Sometimes the most profoundly rooted issues are invisible. They hide deep underground, and people are not always what they seem.

Look at Baron for example. He is a good looking little boy, appears average in every way from a distance. Only when you get close, you can see and feel something different. He doesn't talk to anyone, and he stares straight ahead a lot. Seems like he knows what is going on all around him, but it is not all that important to him. He is aloof and lives in a fully developed inner galaxy. Super smart, he even has some superpowers.

He can communicate telepathically. And Baron observes what is happening at distant places. He calls this remote viewing. He has even teleported things with his mind. It is quite impressive.

Baron doesn't connect with others because it brings his super high energy down and changes the inner equilibrium that keeps him happy. People think that he is not empathetic, but it is not true. Baron just doesn't lower his energy that far down very often. He knows his mother wants him to be "normal," but he would rather be himself, be authentic. That is what makes him happy. He thinks maybe his mother would be more content if she were more authentic and stopped worrying about all her social commitments, all the outer appearances.

Baron's mother, Miriam, is tall with bright blue eyes, long blond hair, and a near perfect body. She continually works at staying beautiful. Several hours a day at the gym and beauty parlor keeps her in excellent condition. Baron's father, James, appreciates it and tells Miriam how attracted he is to her quite often. But they have so little time together.

James, an influential businessman, has been called a captain of industry, whatever that means. Sounds old-fashioned. Even when James is around physically, his attention is not. He is either on the telephone or computer, reading reports from his business. He says that is how they all can live so luxuriously. Maybe a little less luxury and a little more time focused on the family would be better for everyone. That is what Baron thinks.

Miriam wants more connection, more intimacy, less loneliness. James' life is filled with connections. He wants more space to relax and unplug when he has a moment to breathe at home. Baron is glad he has his inner world where he is neither lonely nor needs space. He has struck a perfect balance in the interior realms, he has everything he could ever desire. The outer is superfluous to him, not significant. He says the seeds of everything come from the inner landscape.

At Knock, Miriam came to pray to the Virgin Mary, Queen of Ireland at the site where Mary had appeared in a vision back in 1879 one rainy night around 8 pm. The miraculous apparition floated in place with silent white statuesque figures of Joseph and the Apostle John and Mary for about four hours while it rained all around. The rain was usual in western Ireland, the dry ground under the apparition was not.

Fifteen people who witnessed the scene came forward to courageously declare what they had seen. Revealing religious sentiments at the time of English rule was risky as many attempts to oust Catholic religion from Ireland were in progress. Some attempts had been quite successful. But things were changing. The parish priest had just finished praying a hundred days in a row for the souls in purgatory, and it was the eve of the celebration of the Assumption of Mary, the mother of Christ, into Heaven. Religious fervor was in the air when the apparition of the Blessed Virgin appeared.

On that rainy night, the image at the church gable was so real, one old woman even attempted to kiss the Virgin Mary's feet, but the entire vision retracted as the old woman approached. Since that time, many, many miracles curing deafness, blindness, and other physical ailments including MS have occurred at Knock; even individually healing three visiting Archbishops from Toronto, Tasmania, and Perth, Australia. None have been proven scientifically however, only improving the quality of the lives that were touched.

Miraculously, since the time of the vision in 1879, no famines have plagued Ireland. And while many of the faithful have thrown away their crutches, showing signs of apparent physical healing, it is unknown how many more people have had inner spiritual healing where the effects are not so outwardly dramatic. It would take a massive follow up, and some of the miracle recipients might not be willing to openly share their victory as they hadn't shared their personal struggle.

Lukas laid on one of the beds in the hotel room and continued to read about the history of Knock to learn more about this little-known place, famous in Catholic circles, but relatively unknown outside of that world. Seemed as if Lourdes and Fatima had become much more famous, even among the Irish, probably because the figures in those apparitions spoke while the Knock figures remained silent, merely praying and pointing to heaven.

Only in August of each year does the tiny town throw off her sleepy bed covers and welcome thousands of pilgrims from all over the world. More than 20,000 people descend upon the quiet hamlet each year, normally home to less than 1000 full time residents. Novenas and prayers hoping for untold blessings rule the days and nights. But now it was May, and the little hamlet was quiet.

Baron's mother hoped to make direct intercession with the Virgin Mary for her son. She so wanted, with all her heart that Baron could have a full, beautiful and love-filled life, as any mother desired for her child. However, with all her resources and that of her husband, nothing in the outer world had been able to help. She wept every day for her son. She cried at night for herself.

19

OPENING LUKAS

"Baron, what do you think about all this Knock stuff?" asked Lukas out loud since they were alone in their hotel room.

Baron transferred a thought to Lukas. *"Something is going on here. I don't know exactly what. The energy is very high. It feels holy, but I am not sure it is really for me. Might be just for my Mom. After all, she is the one who is unhappy. Not me. By the way, Lukas, have you thought any more about the Skytalker dude?"*

"From time to time, those guys in the basement of the Rome airport cross my mind. I don't know what to do. My mind is so full of worry about Sofia. And yet I gave my word. But then again, what if they really destroy one-third of the world? Maybe they are better off in the basement. You haven't found anything online about Skytalker, have you?"

"Nope. Nothing too promising. But I do have an idea," said Baron.

"What's that?" asked Lukas.

"Let's open you up and see what you have inside. There may be a clue. After all, with the incantations from Anna and the suitcase gang, you were summoned. Perhaps a clue exists inside of you as to why. Your name is Lukas S. O'Malley. What does the S stand for?"

"Don't think it stands for anything. Heard it was more important to have a middle initial rather than a middle name. S. suits me fine," said Lukas.

"Hmmm. Why, out of all the suitcases in Rome that day, were you the one singled out? There must be a reason. It is inside of you, I am sure."

"What could it be? Sofia's treasures, clothes, and shoes fill me up," said Lukas.

"Humor me," encouraged Baron with his thoughts.

Lukas lay back on the bed. Baron tried to unzip him but came across a lock.

"What's the combination?" asked Baron.

"I don't know. Sofia always handled that."

"Crazy, Lukas. You don't even know how to unlock yourself and look inside!" said Baron in thought.

Baron started moving the combination numbers super-fast like he was working a Rubik's cube when 'pop,' it opened. It was the first time Lukas saw him smile. Just a little upturn of his lips, on the edges but it could be definitely classified as a smile. Usually, Baron's small mouth with thin lips was just a narrow straight line across his face under his nose.

"Ok, Lukas. You are right. Some fancy clothes and some great shoes. Italian style. Nice. Nice purse too. But what are these things?" asked Baron.

Baron pulled out a small crystal singing bowl, a little wooden baton, a small cloth bag that had some incense, a candle, and 3 gold coins with the head of a lion and the name Avalon on the front. On the back side of the coins, a flaming sword between two columns said: "In Freedom's Name".

Before Baron zipped up a now empty Lukas, he noticed the inner lining, light blue in color had the words 'sky blue' woven into the design of the fabric repeatedly. Sky blue, sky blue, sky blue. Or was it blue sky?

Baron stopped and stared out the window. His mind was far away, and yet he was concentrating intensely. Baron could multi-task better than anyone. His brain operated like that of a dolphin; it could do so many things simultaneously, multidimensionally.

Lukas remembered how much Sofia loved each of these items. *She had cured herself of a terrible, little-known auto-immune disorder called poly-arteritis nodosa many years earlier using Reiki and Sound Healing. The doctors had been mystified as their pills and treatments did no good. The invisible realms made all the difference to Sofia's health. The power of gold and freedom also played a role in her health. She used both to raise her vibration.*

Sofia connected her body, mind, and spirit to the invisible by concentrating on stillness, silence, and spaciousness when entering deeply into meditation. Intuition brought balance into her life. She found harmony in her voice and brought that harmony to all her relationships. Sofia laughed often. Her laughter was healing. One time, she instigated laughter on a train going from Rome to Naples. Beginning with a slight giggle, her laughter became infectious, and everyone in her train car laughed with her. So much fun, reminisced Lukas.

Sofia was responsible for the energy she brought to the world. Sometimes, as a Reiki Master, she took on hopeless cases but eventually had to say goodbye when her power got compromised or used up. Many people did not understand her; too happy for them, and they hated it. People did not see Sofia's struggles for she did not readily share that side of herself. She preferred to be a giver rather than a taker. When she needed to replenish, she went into her private cave or found isolated places in nature. There she healed herself.

Earlier in life, she was even a good businesswoman. That had its limits though, as she would never take the easy way out with lies or manipulation. It shortened her career.

By becoming a Reiki Master, Sofia upped her personal energy quotient. After one year of giving herself a Reiki treatment every day, she no longer had any symptoms of the autoimmune disorder that had plagued her. Just two years earlier, Sofia had been looking at either an early death or the possibility of a very sedentary life in a wheelchair. Neither of those timelines developed.

Instead, Sofia left corporate life behind, went to Mexico, met Angelo, opened a bakery/restaurant and a Reiki Center. This began an incredibly exciting time in her life. At the bakery/restaurant, Sofia transferred her corporate marketing skills and a passion for cooking into making delicious pastries which she imbued with Reiki energy. People reported how great they felt after eating at her place. Soon her restaurant was so popular that she closed her Reiki center and focused entirely on serving delicious food. Reiki always went into the food and Reiki classes were taught when there was time. Sofia honored the Full Moon each month by going to the beach and doing ceremonies with her spiritual friends.

Full moon ceremonies began by calling in the four directions, the elements, the guardians of the place, the cosmos and mother earth as a Mayan Shaman had taught her. Each person in the circle then became a loving channel for cosmic energy to connect to earth energy through them. Each, then, was offered an opportunity to pray, sing, dance, chant or express their deepest feelings in the group setting before closing the circle with hugs and well wishes. The purest and most natural form of spiritual communion in front of the full moon formed Sofia's calling card so that when people in the little town thought of the moon, they thought of her.

Life with Angelo was passionate. Sofia and Angelo both worked hard, fought with each other often as the differences in their ages, cultures, and temperaments took center stage. But then they also made passionate love all along the coast of the Riviera Maya and beyond. Some weekends, I traveled with Sofia and Angelo too. It was fun, sexy and exhilarating, always.

Sofia stayed in the moment with everything and everyone but the driving desire to re-open her Reiki center in the jungle remained in the background. She and Angelo were finally at a good point financially with their restaurant empire for Sofia to devote herself to her spiritual practices and less to business. Angelo told her flat out that he wasn't interested. His only interest besides tennis was business.

Sofia was crushed. She had put her dreams and plans on hold to help Angelo achieve his goals. He now had his sailboat and a financial platform to sail into old age, but he had no interest in helping her reach her dreams. Perhaps they had spent too much time together, working hard and being together every day for so many hours a day. It took a toll on each of them. Space was needed between them.

Sofia longed to share her profound connection to the spiritual world with Angelo. In the early days of the relationship, they shared everything. Sofia felt she had been an excellent partner to Angelo, but he wanted nothing to do with the spiritual life. He said he was happy to be firmly planted upon the earth.

Angelo loved Sofia in his own way but was unwilling to give her what she most desired. The two of them came to an impasse. Neither one understood the other any longer. And neither one was willing to incorporate the other's point of view into theirs. A clash of inner titans broke them apart. Life had other plans for their love.

Sofia made her way on her own in the world. Faithful to her spiritual self on her inner life's journey, even at the expense of giving up her relationship with Angelo, she incorporated a traveling cure into her life.

Sofia found Asia. She hiked the Himalayas and the outer islands of Hong Kong, she thrived on the banks of the Chao Phraya River and shopped the weekend market in Bangkok. She prayed in the flower-laden temples of Bali, loving it all. Sofia found Buddhism in Bhutan and began to meditate. Basically, she turned down the outer flame of her life as she turned inward. Eventually, Sofia closed all her businesses with Angelo and began to write poetry, practice energy healing with dolphins and do qigong.

Angelo invited her to his son's wedding in Italy this year. They had a great time, a really great time. It seemed like a romance was sparking up once again. We were all returning to Cancun from the wedding when I got separated from them. Now you know almost everything, Baron, said Lukas.

"Hmmmm, more than you know, Lukas. More than you can even imagine."

20

BARON AND THE BOWL

"Lukas, this crystal bowl keeps calling to me to be played. It feels like it is alive. Let's see what it wants to say. Let's peek into what is really inside of you. Get comfortable. I am going to play the bowl," said Baron.

But Baron, we have just taken everything out of me, said Lukas.

"Oh, Lukas, we have only taken Sofia's things out. You now have space inside. It is like a blue sky. It says so on your inner lining. Focus on that. Just get comfortable and close your eyes."

Lukas lay back on the bed and took a deep breath and relaxed. He noticed that his right nostril was dominant.

Baron lit the candle and incense, placed the bowl on the floor and sat in front of it. He took a deep breath and paused a moment, then closed his eyes. A moment later, Baron took the little wooden baton, gently bounced it on the outside of the rim of the crystal bowl twice. He then began moving the wand around the edges of the bowl in a circular pattern. A most fantastic sound came emerged, just like when Sofia plays.

The sound seemed to take on an invisible gelatinous form and surround Lukas like one end of a figure eight. It crossed back over at the bowl and enveloped Baron with the other end of a figure eight. They had all become one thing - Baron, the crystal bowl, and Lukas in the form of an energetic infinity symbol. The sound seemed to lift them up like they were hovering over the floor. Lukas felt so free, so happy and then felt like he was flying.

He knew the bowl sounds were continuing, but he began to see things in his mind's eye. First, he saw the little boy named Luke Skytalker. Lukas went to the little boy's house. The little boy and his friends joined together to say, 'Please remember to smile' with the emphasis on the word smile, at the end of their YouTube videos. But Lukas knew intuitively that the little boy was not the one that Anna and the suitcases were looking for. They needed someone who could introduce the space element to their conundrum.

Lukas heard himself asking, *what is the space element?* When whoosh... he flew out of the little boys' house and began flying again, this time under a bright blue sky. It was one of those blue, blue skies where you don't notice the color of anything else because the blue is so intense. Lukas landed in a field and laid back on a luscious cushion of green grass and wildflowers. He stared at the sky.

Lukas watched as a tiny, wispy white cloud formed then dissipated. Then another, then another. He had never noticed before that the sky was extraordinarily active during what seemed to be a bright, sunny day. Pretty soon, Lukas observed a big fluffy white cloud arrive on the left-hand side of his visual field. It floated to the center and remained there for a long time before it moved on. A slow-motion show in what appeared, at first glance, to be an empty clear sky. Relaxed, breathing deeply and slowly, Lukas noted Baron's bowl playing in the background.

He remembered Karma saying something about our thoughts, worries, and emotions being like clouds in the sky. They show up, stay for a while and then leave. Lukas embodied this idea. Now he really knew what Karma meant. This was so cool.

Lukas heard Baron stop playing the bowl but didn't want to leave the serenity of the moment. So, he stayed breathing deep for a long time without moving. Lukas seemed to be able to follow the end of the sound from the bowl into the inaudible part of the electromagnetic spectrum. A knock at the hotel room door snapped him out of the reverie and brought him back to the Irish hotel room.

"Baron, it is time to go. You have fifteen minutes to get ready," said the male voice through the door.

Lukas opened his eyes and looked at Baron. He could swear that Baron made eye contact with him and was smiling. Lukas smiled too.

"Come on, Lukas. Let's get ready," said Baron in silence as he put the crystal bowl and the baton on the table.

"Can you bring me with you to the church?" Lukas asked out loud.

"Sure, why not?" Baron was now staring straight ahead again.

"Well, you know, I am a suitcase," said Lukas.

"No one will mind. Just watch. The adults are used to my eccentric ways and generally tolerate what I want to do. Just brush that road dust off you and get ready to go."

2 1

THE BASILICA

"Baron, why are you wheeling a suitcase with you?" asked the male voice. It wasn't his father's voice but rather the resonant sound of his manservant, Godfrey.

Baron stopped walking and stared straight ahead. He held more tightly onto Lukas hoping Godfrey realized it was essential to bring the suitcase with them.

Baron's mother, stopped, looked at a smudge on his face. She pulled out a lace hanky, wet it with her mouth and wiped Baron's cheek clean as some mother's do. "It's ok Godfrey. Let him bring it with him. I think it is making him feel surer of himself," said Miriam.

As they all entered the limo, Baron's father was talking on his cell phone. The overcast sky hung above with heavy grey moisture-laden clouds, and the wind was blowing, but the cold was kept at bay. Miriam dressed in a pearly white knee-length dress had her royal blue rosary beads in her hand. They matched nicely with her two-toned blue and pearl white shoes. Stunning, as usual. Baron's father sent an admiring glance her way as they got out of the car at the Basilica.

Miriam and James had requested a private mass for their son months earlier. For that, they stopped in the rector's office before going into the church. Father Brian had been James' business colleague before he gave up business to dedicate his life to God as a priest about 10 years earlier. Now, because Father Brian had been so successful in administering whatever project the Church gave him, the Archdiocese rewarded him with one of the most important churches in Ireland, the Basilica at Knock.

Today, celebrating the holy sacrifice of the mass at the Basilica for Baron and his family proved to be a remarkable day for all of them.

"Hi, Brian. Good to see you again." James shook Father Brian's hand.

"Hello everyone. So, this is Baron. What a handsome lad," said Father Brian.

Baron stared straight ahead as usual.

"What do you say, let's get on with the mass. Go ahead in and sit wherever you like. It is a private mass, but we never close the doors to anyone who would like to join in. I hope you understand. We are extremely grateful for your generous donation to our efforts here James," said Father Brian.

The family seated themselves in front of the altar. One of the most beautiful mosaics ever created was directly behind the altar which stood in the center of the Basilica. Huge, 14 meters by 14 meters, it depicted the miraculous apparition that had occurred at the old parish church gable in Knock almost a hundred forty years earlier. The stunning mosaic artistry of Mary, the Queen of Heaven pictured her with a golden crown while looking heavenward. The palms of her hands faced each other as if she was holding enormous energy between her hands. St. Joseph, on bended knee with hands in prayer position behind Mary to the left, looked down in a gaze of sincere and profound prayer and reverence. To Mary's right, slightly behind her and a little lower was the figure of St John the Evangelist with a book in his left hand. The first two fingers of his right hand pointing up to the heavens as if he was saying this is divine knowledge. Some say John was the author of Revelations in the Bible.

The whole mosaic enveloped in a golden light drew one's attention in. To the right of the three figures, an altar with a white lamb upon it sat in front of a large cross behind. Angels flanked either side and above. Again, a golden white light highlighted everything. Stunning.

The mosaic outlined in distinctive detail the fifteen people who had come forward to declare what they had seen; they were in various stages of awe and prayer looking at the beatific vision. A few more figures said to have been at the church at the time of the apparition but did not dare to come forward for fear of reprisal rounded out mosaic depicted as figures with few discernible features.

Designed by an Irishman, manufactured and partially joined together by Italians, the mosaic then made its journey to Ireland where it was assembled like a jigsaw puzzle. The completed masterpiece had some sort of beautiful, powerful energy, akin to deep presence, coming from it in the center of the large basilica. Perhaps the reflection of all the people who had prayed before this centerpiece of the Basilica imbued it with the qualities of hope and adoration.

Father Brian entered ceremoniously with two altar boys in attendance to begin the mass. A few older parishioners had heard about the special private ceremony. Never really any secrets around that church, the old ones made their way in but sat apart from the family on the other side of the altar. After Father Brian finished giving everyone Holy Communion, he looked at the family and said, "I invite each of you to come up individually to receive a blessing on the altar, if you so desire."

Miriam arose and grabbed Baron's hand. He quickly slid his slender hand out from her white glove but took hold of Lukas and followed her to the altar. Godfrey closed the end of the procession as James walked to the back of the church to talk on his phone.

"Miriam, what would you like to pray for," asked Father Brian.

"Oh Father, I ask for the intercession of the holy Virgin Mother that she have mercy on my son and upon me. I ask that she forgive me for anything I may have ever done wrong and to please bring my son what he needs for health and happiness."

"So be it." Father Brian raised his eyes heavenward and making the sign of the cross, began to pray, "In the name of the Father, the Son, and the Holy Spirit. Dear Holy Mother, please hear this woman's prayers. Restore her and her son to wholeness, holiness. May they shed any of the slings and arrows of those who hate, have envy or jealousy toward them. And may they go forward from this day at one with your true love and compassion for humanity. May this all be done by you through me in this holy place in the Basilica at Knock, sealed by the love of our Lord, your holy Son, the Lamb of God, now and forever more. Amen."

Miriam said, "Amen." She turned to take Baron's hand but again he slid it out of her glove. He moved closer to the priest and handed him his iPad. Miriam returned to her seat.

On the iPad Baron had written, *please pray for me and my suitcase named Lukas and his friend, Sofia.*

Father Brian smiled. "Ok," he said. "In the name of the Father, the Son, and the Holy Spirit. Dear Lady, Mother of our Lord, Queen of Ireland, Queen of the Universe. Here before you, a child has asked for your kindness, your compassion, your prayers to restore him, his friend, Lukas and their friend Sofia to complete wholeness, holiness. In your infinite wisdom, please hear our prayers and grant the blessings needed this very day for each and every one of them. We thank you in advance, knowing it is already done. Amen."

Baron nodded his head without making eye contact, took his iPad with one hand and Lukas by the handle with the other and went back to his seat.

Godfrey then approached Father Brian. "Dear Father, I would like to pray for everyone in the world who has suffered trauma, whether it is personal violence, trauma caused by natural disasters like earthquakes, hurricanes, fires, and floods, or wars or even political hatred and racism. I know many people affected by trauma and would like to pray for all of them. Also, please ask the Holy Mother to ask God to forgive me for all my sins."

"That is an essential and powerful prayer. What did you say your name was?"

"Godfrey. Godfrey Godfree."

"Let us pray, Godfrey Godfree. In the name of the Father, the Son, and the Holy Spirit. Dear Mary, Mother of God, please have mercy on your children, all who suffer the senseless arrows of hate and trauma, whatever form it may take, whether it is natural disasters, war, terrorism, hate crimes or even traditional bullying. Please erase the effects of the suffering from their past, present, and future. Balance and wash clean their memories so that the traumas cease now as a bad dream stops when one awakes. May these traumas no longer affect their ability to love you and serve you in the name of the Lord most high and by the grace of all the angels of heaven. Amen."

As Father Brian finished praying with Godfrey, he raised his two hands above Godfrey's head. He traced along both sides of Godfrey's body as if it was a candle flame as he said, "May you be forgiven of all your sins in the name of Mary and her precious son, Jesus Christ."

We all saw Godfrey tremble slightly. When opened, his two-toned brown eyes glistened. He thanked Father Brian and went to his seat.

James was still in the back of the church on the phone as Father Brian finished the mass. A beautiful Irish woman's voice came from behind us on the speaker system singing as Father Brian, and his two altar boys bowed before the cross and left the altar in procession.

The group sat in the pew for quite a while after the beautiful voice stopped singing. No one wanted to move and let this pristine moment pass into eternity. The few old people sitting on the other side left the Basilica. Bits and pieces of James' conversation could be heard seeping into the silence from the back of the church.

Godfrey was the first to speak. He stared straight ahead and said, "Wow! I felt a powerful wave of energy flow through me when Father Brian traced his hands along the outside of my body. It was electrifying," he said. "I am sure everyone who has experienced trauma will be helped by his powerful prayers today. This makes me so happy; I feel clean on so many levels," said Godfrey.

Miriam turned to him and said, "Thank you for being with us today, Godfrey. You have been so important in Baron's life since day one. It is only right and fitting that you be here now and receive the blessings with us."

Her blue eyes were also glistening, but there was something different about them. It seemed as if now a light like a candle playing in the breeze shone in her eyes. More beautiful than before, she didn't appear to be 38 but much younger.

"Ms. Miriam, I feel so blessed to be a part of your family, to know you and Baron. My life is so much the better for it. Thank you from the center of my heart," said Godfrey.

Baron was staring at the mosaic. Even though he never shows emotion, Lukas thought he saw a little something at the edge of Baron's eye. Not wanting to intrude in on his moment here, Lukas thought he would wait until they were alone later in the hotel to talk about all of this.

Just then, James appeared. "So, how did it all go? Everyone happy?"

Everyone nodded, except Baron, who still looked straight ahead at the mural.

22

TALKING

"You know, there are really 1,800,422 pieces in the mosaic," said Baron, out loud in the hotel room.

"Did you count them all?" asked Lukas.

"Yes, I did."

"Wow. And now you are talking? Is this a miracle, Baron?"

"Not really, I could always talk but didn't want to, so I didn't."

"Why?" asked Lukas.

"Most conversations bore me. Have you ever really listened to what people talk about on a daily basis? Weather, food, fashion, gossip, problems with other people, shocking news stories that may or may not be true. Politics. Nothing beneficial and extremely boring to me."

"So, you just stopped talking?" asked Lukas.

"Yes, and that was when I started observing the world in incredible detail. You can learn anything if you pay attention to the details. But you need mental space to be able to concentrate on the details. If you are always talking to people, you fill up your head with chatter, and you will never learn anything."

"Wow, Baron. Thank you for talking to me," said Lukas.

"You are different, Lukas. For one thing, you listen and know how to do thought transference. Where did you learn that?"

"Ha! In the basement of the Rome airport from Anna and the Four Horsemen suitcases. In fact, I think I have to get back to them soon. Mary, the Queen in the mural spoke to me during the time Father Brian was praying for us."

"She did?" asked Baron. "What did she say?"

"She told me that I should help the Four Horsemen suitcases. She said it was more important than I could imagine. She told me to study the mosaic, and I would realize why."

"Hmmm... Do you think she knows something about Skytalker that we don't?" asked Baron.

"I don't know, but I am getting the feeling that this whole thing is bigger than we know. Maybe the meaning behind it is not one that is commonly known or accepted."

"Here I took a photo of the mural with my iPad while we were in the Basilica. Let's look at it."

Baron and Lukas looked at the photo for a long time without saying anything to each other.

"Lukas, you know some people say everything written about the Apocalypse already happened during Roman times. Others say it is really about the classic struggle between good and evil where good always wins but the struggle never ends."

"Really? I wonder why those Four Horsemen suitcases are so anxious to get out of the airport basement. They really believe they are gearing up to change the world by destroying it."

"Who wouldn't want to get out of the cellar?" said Baron. "You wanted out, didn't you Lukas?"

"Well, yeah but that was different. I wanted to get back to Sofia and Cancun. Know what, though, I am beginning to feel a little different about that now too. Something important is pulling me away from my old ideas. I don't yet know what it is exactly. But I must let go. Let go of Sofia."

Lukas paused and looked out the window at a slight patch of blue in the sky. The sun was trying to come out, but the clouds held their heaviness. A blue spot drew in Lukas' focus and attention. He stared at it like Baron often stares. Calmness and spaciousness established themselves inside of him.

"Baron, I never thought I could feel like this. Something has changed. I am wondering if we can pack up Sofia's things that we took out of me and mail them to Mexico. What do you think? Her address is on this luggage tag here. Maybe Godfrey can help us?"

"Wow, Lukas. Sounds like a miracle moved through you," said Baron still speaking out loud.

"Oh, don't get me wrong, Baron. I still love Sofia with all my heart and would be so happy to see her again. But something is different inside of me now. I know I have something significant to accomplish. My life, all of our lives depend upon it."

"Ok, let's get Godfrey to help us," said Baron.

23

GODFREY

A tall man with a slow gait, Godfrey didn't seem to fit in with any sort of typical description. A big, muscular, man with sandy blond, greying hair, ruddy complexion and brown wide-set eyes on a squarish, yet oval face that gave him a baby look on an over six-foot tall frame. You could call him lanky with an uncommon grace when he walked. It wasn't the usual long, lank step you would expect of someone tall, and lean like him. He seemed to glide when he walked, like a dancer. Godfrey somehow defies exact description as he always changes, even slightly. It's hard to say what that change is all about. Godfrey is a fluid person, yeah, that's the best way to describe him, fluid. No sharp edges.

An incredibly beautiful power comes from Godfrey. You can feel it when he walks in the room. He is the perfect bodyguard/manservant. He can even become invisible if he wants to, all six feet 2 inches of him. It is one of his superpowers. We all have something.

A quiet man in his late 40s, Godfrey reads a lot, but I don't think his life was always so quiet. He doesn't talk much about himself, at the same time, he doesn't seem to miss a detail of what is going on around him; acutely aware and quite smart.

"Baron, do you ever talk with Godfrey?" asked Lukas.

"He knows about thought transference, so we don't have to talk. He said his cat taught him how to do it."

"Wow, smart cat."

"Most cats are smart. Didn't you say that Sofia had a cat?" Baron's voice was getting more powerful all the time, now that he was using it."

"Yeah, Fernando. He is a big golden red cat depending on who you talk to. Some say he is blond others say red. Perhaps he is what is called strawberry blonde. Fernando speaks in so many ways... with his eyes, a flick of his tail, rubbing his head on you and he even smacks his lips when he wants to eat. So funny. Occasionally, he will use his voice."

"I still remember the day he went outside with a little kitty meow voice and came back with a deep adult MEOW voice. Never knew what happened on that day but his voice never went back to the little meow. So shocking and cool to be aware of that moment, Sofia and I laughed a lot about that one."

"Awareness is king," agreed Baron. "Godfrey is coming. Let's ask him to mail Sofia's stuff to her. I will explain."

Godfrey knocked on the door and entered the room. Baron looked at Godfrey in the eye and then looked away to stare out the window. Godfrey nodded his head and began to gather Sofia's things.

Godfrey, thought Lukas.

Yes? he answered in thought.

Thank you so much for doing this. I really appreciate it. But please leave the crystal bowl, baton and little bag of things. I will explain it to Sofia another time. She will understand, Lukas thought in silence.

Okay, whatever you say, Lukas. Godfrey replied silently.

With that, Godfrey left the room with Sofia's things in his arms. A twinge of sadness at the emptiness inside popped up in Lukas. Then he realized this was precisely what was needed, and Sofia was going to be okay.

"Baron, do you think Sofia will think of me anymore?" asked Lukas.

"Sure, she will."

"I hope she realizes that I have something crucial and compelling to do. All women, not just Sofia, and the whole world depend on me. I have a mission, a purpose for being."

24

THE GAYATRI MANTRA

Lukas began to play the crystal bowl for Baron this time. Baron closed his eyes and swayed with the clockwise circular sounds as if he was becoming one with the vibration.

"Om bhoor bhuvaha, swaha. Om tat savitur varenyam. Bhargo divasya dimahi. Di yoyo naha. Prechodiat, Om," he chanted as he played.

Lukas learned this chant during his time in the basement of the Rome Airport. Wayan told him it is called the Gayatri Mantra, and it praises Infinite Intelligence as the primordial sound with no beginning or end who blesses through the breath of the Divine Will. Infinite Intelligence has absolute consciousness and is more significant than space, grander than the blue sky. Infinite Intelligence is omnipresent and is inside and outside of all physical things. Infinite Intelligence is the source of all things. Those who are worthy to receive the glorious light of Infinite Intelligence's love and power are satisfied by it in a way that no earthly thing can fulfill. It is so pure that just being in the presence of Infinite Intelligence can purify anyone or anything. Focusing on Infinite Intelligence and meditating often with both our hearts and minds has the potential to uplift each of us and all of humanity. By asking not only for guidance and inspiration but to also remove the darkness of Maya from our paths, we may encounter the source of pure bliss, the peace of God, Infinite Intelligence.

The sound current pulled Lukas into it as the sun peaked out from the dense clouds before it set for the day. It was a lovely way to end the afternoon, full of peace, full of bliss.

25

⤫

THE GARDAI

Godfrey passed by a room in the hotel filled with police officers. He glanced in and kept walking with his arms overflowing with women's clothes and shoes. He put them in his room and left to find a box big enough to send it all to Mexico.

The hotel had already disposed of the daily trash, so Godfrey enlisted the help of the limo driver to take him for a ride to find a box. It was raining and cold when they arrived at Flanagan's pub in the little Irish village of Brickens nearby.

Brickens was named for freckle-faced people built like badgers. A couple of them were in the pub drinking pints of Guinness with their mothers, watching Gaelic football on the telly. Seemed to be a family thing as they all had freckles and looked alike.

While Godfrey and the limo driver enjoyed a snack, the barkeep found a box for them. Flanagan's offered typical Irish bar food, like roast beef and mashed potatoes and salmon and chips in addition to some exciting fusion dishes like Spanish Tapas with Irish bacon and hot sauce. Come to find out, the barkeep was culinary school trained but preferred the company of drinkers to that of the stove and the oven. Rather talkative, especially about food and Gaelic football, he invited Godfrey and the limo driver back again.

Later, at the hotel, Godfrey had just finished packing up Sofia's clothes when there was a knock at his hotel room door. The Irish police, the Gardai, wanted to talk with him.

"What can I do to help you, gentlemen?" Godfrey asked looking calm but feeling jittery inside.

"There was a little problem down the hall. A woman was violently raped sometime between midnight and noon. We are trying to figure out exactly what happened. Did you hear or see anything?" asked the Gardai officer.

"No, sir. I was in the Basilica with the Von Camerberg family this morning," answered Godfrey.

"Oh, you were. Ok. What time was that?"

"It was between 10 am and noon. I didn't pay attention to the exact time we returned. Then I went to Flanagan's Pub in Brickens this afternoon. What happened?" asked Godfrey.

"We are trying to find out more. Where were you last night?"

"Hmmm. After dinner, I went to the Pub here in the hotel and listened to the music. Then I went to bed early around 10:30 pm. I am a heavy sleeper. Didn't hear anything. Sorry," said Godfrey.

"One of the officers commented that you passed by the room with an armload of women's clothes. What was that all about?" asked the officer.

"Oh, that. The young lad I help care for asked me to mail them to his friend in Mexico. Would you like her name?" asked Godfrey.

"No, no. That is fine, but I would like to take your name, address and phone number if you don't mind. The young lady is unconscious in the hospital right now. What did you say your name was?"

"Godfrey. Godfrey Godfree."

"Ok, Mr. Godfree. We will call you if we have any more questions. If you think of anything to help us, please call. Here is my card."

Police always make me nervous, thought Godfrey as he finished addressing the box to Sofia. *I still remember the day they arrested me and put me in jail in Florida. It was in front of that bookstore in West Palm Beach.*

Just sitting on the bench under a palm tree I was enjoying the day, minding my own business. Ok, I was a little high but nothing major, just some pot, when like a swarm of wasps, the police descended upon me, knocked me to the ground yelling the whole time. I didn't know what was going on and started fighting back. I think I punched a couple of them and gave them black eyes before they subdued me with stun guns. It was all so strange.

They dragged me to their squad car, brought me to jail and charged me with robbing the bookstore. I couldn't believe it. An hour earlier, I had been in the bookstore but didn't find anything I wanted to read, so I went outside and smoked a joint. The police said they had me on camera, full proof that I had robbed the bookstore.

"Hey, I know my rights. I want to make a phone call," I told them.

"Here, go ahead," said the police officer as she handed me the phone.

I called my mom who lived close by. "Hi, Mom. I need your help."

"Godfrey, where are you, honey?"

"Mom, at the police station in West Palm. They arrested me," said Godfrey.

"What did you do, son?"

"Nothing, Mom. I just minded my own business, sitting in the park in front of the bookstore, enjoying the day when the police came, knocked me to the ground and arrested me. They say I robbed the bookstore. I didn't do it," said Godfrey.

"Oh, Honey. I am going to fix my face and come to see you right away. Don't worry. Sit tight, sweetheart."

With that, my mother started calling my sisters, all four of them. And they talked her out of coming to see me.

I can just hear them repeating the same thing. "Mom, you know Godfrey has been getting messed up with drugs, he is on the wrong path in life, and he has no money for rehab. Let him get dried out in jail."

I waited all day. My mom never arrived.

The next day I made another call.

"Mom, I thought you said you were coming to see me. What happened?"

"Oh honey, your sisters convinced me to leave you there. You know you have been having trouble with the drink and the drugs. Maybe it will do you good to clean up your act."

"Oh Mom, but I didn't rob the bookstore. It is mistaken identity," said Godfrey.

"Oh Honey. Take advantage of the situation. Get your life on track. I will check if I can come to see you tomorrow. Can I bring you anything?"

"Yes, please bring me some toothpaste and deodorant," I pleaded.

I was distraught. My mother had always been there for me, and now, even she left me. Here I was in jail with a whole host of nasty, dirty, smelly people, you know the ones who live under the bridges and in the parks. Those who walk around with shopping carts filled with all their earthly belongings in bags. I guess when they are not walking around free and living in the public bathrooms, they live in the jails especially in Florida.

My cellmate was from Jamaica. He was a preacher and said that he, too, was in on mistaken identity. How can this be that they even arrest a preacher? What kind of craziness is this? I wondered if the Florida sun was getting to the policemen's heads. Maybe they needed better hats."

Laying on my bed, I began shaking and shivering as all the drugs I had been using were calling for more? I was on the bottom bunk. I had no money, no real friends, and even my family would not help me. I cried, I thrashed, I wailed, I sweated hot, I sweated cold. I wanted to jump out of my skin, but there was nowhere to go. The preacher came over and covered me with a blanket.

I fell asleep and had a dream. I think it was a dream, it was so real, it might have been a hallucination, but I will call it a dream. In it, a beast with ten heads was fighting with me. Each time, I cut off a head with my sword, two more would grow. Finally, I learned to just maim the heads, then the beast would slow down.

In the dream, running through the woods I hid behind large rocks, in caves, and behind trees but the beast would always find me. One time, I watched from behind a rock near a still pool of water as the beast turned into a beautiful woman and began to call me. If I hadn't seen it with my own two eyes, I would have fallen for the trick. Luckily, I became aware and developed a plan.

I asked the woman to walk with me through the woods. She told me about the story of her life. Her name was Legacy. She told me about all the traumas of her life, that of her mother, aunts, grandmothers and even women who were friends of the family or noted members of the community. All she wanted to talk about was trauma inflicted upon women of all times. Such a downer, it seemed as if each ordeal was more terrible than the others. Vicious rapes, emotional abuse, sexual slavery of women and girls chained to beds all populated her talk track. She even talked about some little boys going through what women go through. Through the DNA, the ancestry, all women would continue to suffer from trauma.

"Trauma is not all bad if you use it well," she said. "It seems to make our world go around. You know, it is easier to control someone if they are trauma-tized. It is called PTSD, the modern-day ball and chain, the perfect prison without walls."

She continued, "Someone had to pay for Lucifer's fall from heaven. He decided it was to be the women. In the Bible, it is spelled out in the story of the Garden of Eden that women were cursed to suffer pain in childbirth because Eve ate the apple supposedly given to her by the serpent. It was in that moment the problems between men and women began. When questioned about the apple, Adam pointed the finger at Eve, trying to save his own skin and even insinuating that God was at fault for giving him a partner that could be so deceived. But that is not the full picture.

Women are powerful. Women are wise. Women, if not closely controlled will change this world and return it to the Garden status, and that is a problem for us. To this day, women still pay for the Fall, through me. I am their Legacy, and I pass the PTSD and the trauma down through the DNA. No one can escape it. Both men and women are damned, but it always comes through the matrilineal line. You can count on it."

At that moment, the woman turned into the beast once again and pinned me against a rock. She/he was about to kill me, strangling me with claws digging deeply into my neck as my larynx was being crushed when a colossal angel swooped down and struck the beast in the heart with his cobalt blue flaming sword. The creature fell back screaming into some sulfur tar pits and sunk away.

I caught my breath in a moment of silence and asked, "Who are you?" as I stared at the bright angel with the sword.

"I am Michael and you, my friend, have some important work to accomplish. Once and for all, you must get off these drugs and stop the drink. Understand?" he said with what sounded like an Irish accent.

Michael's flaming sword now sheathed, hung at his side.

"Wow... okay, Michael. Thank you for saving my life."

"Godfrey, you are worth it," said the angel.

With that, I woke up drenched in sweat to see the preacher man praying over me. His worried face lit up with an instant smile. "You made it," he said in his lilting Jamaican accent.

"Yeah. I wasn't sure about that a few minutes ago, but now I am," said Godfrey.

I, Godfrey Godfree, began reading the Bible for the first time in my life and I haven't picked up drugs or alcohol since.

The next day, my mother came to visit but said she didn't have the money to bail me out. She forgot to bring the deodorant too. So, I stayed the full 30 days awaiting my hearing, as smelly as the rest. But each day I felt stronger, brighter. The Jamaican preacher and I became good friends. I even started developing a Jamaican accent when I talked Bible stuff. Not bad for a good ole boy from New Orleans.

On the 30th day, I went to court. Mom was there waiting with and for me. You should have seen the surprise on her face when the judge threw out the charges for "mistaken identity."

The Lord works in mysterious ways. Must get this box posted to Mexico. We leave back to Rome in the morning.

26

BACK TO ROME

Godfrey pulled the small steaming too hot cup of espresso away from his lips quickly as Baron and Lukas chatted silently. Still not accustomed to the steam after all these years in Italy. Late afternoon in the Rome airport was busy with travelers. Baron's parents had gone on ahead while Godfrey attended to the luggage and to Baron.

Baron, I am not sure what the best plan is. I want to help the suitcases downstairs, but I don't want to risk getting stuck in the basement again, explained Lukas in silence.

"*Lukas, do you know who you really are?*" asked Baron in silence because they were in a public place.

Oh my God, Baron. Now you sound like Karma. Know what, I have the potential to be anyone, anything. My identity, large and fluid, changes, especially since I took Sofia's belongings out from inside of me. I have more room, I have space. I can feel me. I can feel who I am from the inside out, said Lukas.

"*Lukas, you are much greater than you know,*" said Baron.

Really, Baron? Why do you say that?

"*The name imprinted inside. It said Lukas S. O'Malley,*" said Baron

So what? I already know that. I told you, I just have an initial.

"*Lukas, I don't think that is true. All inside of you is the word Sky. It* is imprinted into the light blue fabric inside of you. Sky, sky, sky, blue sky," said Baron.

What are you saying Baron? You think my middle name is Sky?

"Well, I can't say that you are Sky Talker, but I do know you are Sky inside, in the middle," said Baron.

I do feel different ever since we took Sofia's belongings out. Maybe that is why Anna and the others' magic pulled me in because my name is really Lukas Sky O'Malley. But I am a suitcase, said Lukas in silence.

"Have you really gone back to that, Lukas?" asked Baron in silence, staring blankly straight ahead.

Lukas paused for a moment, trying on the thought. *Could I really be Skytalker and not know it? Or maybe just Sky? I have been so wrapped up with Sofia, her life, and her belongings for so long. Maybe I forgot who I really am? Can this be true? It's true that I love Sofia and have traveled with her everywhere for many years. She chooses where we go. She decides what we carry with us and pays for everything. I go along for the ride in the story of her life. I know lots of suitcases who do the same. It is just how it is. We don't get to choose. Maybe I got so wrapped up in Sofia's life that I forgot I also have an independent existence. Wow. Can this be true? I have an identity without Sofia?*

I am so happy when she is happy, and I never think about what I need. Sofia does take good care of me. She cleans me, makes sure my wheels are oiled and even takes me out of the closet every now and then to put me outside in the sunshine and fresh air. I have had a good life.

But I wonder if I was born to do more, be more. I have sky imprinted inside. Is it possible that I need to activate the sky inside and let it talk? Step into being a skytalker? Lukas Skytalker? Luke Skytalker? Or am I a Skywalker? Skygazer? Skydancer? Maybe I am just like the sky? No talking, no walking, no gazing, no dancing. Solo sky.

Baron stared out the window at a patch of blue sky. He pulled Lukas close to him, so he could see too. Lukas stared unblinkingly at the blue Roman sky for a long time with Baron. A shaft of light shone in upon them. At that moment Lukas realized there was no difference between him and the sky. He felt spacious and beautiful inside and out.

Baron, I finally know who I am. I am Luke Sky.

"What?" asked Baron, not really following for the first time ever.

Baron, we all have identities. We choose what feels right, most natural but at the end of the day, it is only an identity. At the very base of everything, we are pure potential. And the sky represents that potential. Right now, I am learning to walk and talk in a way that will bring spaciousness to every heart alive. This is the answer to the conundrum the horseman brought me. I am Sky. Lukas Sky.

"Whatever, Lukas. Quite frankly I have lost your train of thought but must go home now. Do you want to come with Godfrey and me or do you want us to bring you somewhere?" asked Baron.

Can you leave me near where you found me? I have to find my way back to the gang, said Lukas.

"That was Departures, Lukas. We are now in Arrivals. How about if we leave you near Sorelli's Pizza?" asked Baron.

Sounds like a plan. I am going to miss you, Baron. You have helped me recover myself, my life. I will never forget you. Thank you.

"Lukas, we will see each other again. Remember these numbers 366133116336."

What are those Baron? asked Lukas.

"Those are my remote viewing coordinates. If you ever need me or want to talk with me, close your eyes and focus on those numbers until you feel me. The moment you feel me, we are connected to a fantastic inner grid. Then we can communicate freely and easily."

Wow, Baron. You are the best! Lukas wanted to hug him, but he knew Baron didn't like to be touched, so they said goodbye at Sorelli's by nodding at each other. Godfrey and Baron walked away.

27

THE AIRPORT GANG

Seemed like an eternity that Lukas waited in the corner of Sorelli's near the kitchen door. The janitor came by with his mop but only pushed Lukas to the side a short distance.

Damn, Lukas thought. *Now that I want him to send me to the basement he doesn't. Why does life happen like this? Is this another lesson in patience? In waiting? I am sick of it.*

"Pssst."

Lukas looked around but saw nothing.

"Pssst, is that you Lukas?"

"Who wants to know?" asked Lukas, going back to answering questions with questions.

"It's me, Peachie."

"Peachie! I'm back. Can you show me how to get downstairs?" asked Lukas.

"Oh Lukas, I knew you would be back," Peachie squealed with glee. "Here, grab a couple of pizzas and follow me."

Lukas looked left and looked right. Coast was clear, so he spun, grabbed two large anchovy pizzas and zipped behind Peachie.

"Hold on tight, Lukas. We are going down a long tube," said Peachie. Down they went.

THUMP, THUMP, THUMP

Anna wheeled up. For the first time ever, she smiled at Lukas.

"Lukas!" Her voice had lost its snarl. She now sounded smooth like black velvet in the dark.

"Hi, Anna," said Lukas.

"Did you find what you were looking for, big boy?" Anna purred.

"I did and was it a surprise," said Lukas

"Well, where is he?" Anna asked. "Where is Luke Skytalker?"

"Skytalker doesn't exist. You must have gotten your wires crossed, Anna. Maybe your memory failed, or you were a victim of fake news. Skytalker is a complete fantasy, a YouTube video, nothing more," said Lukas.

Anna started to cry. "Don't tell me this, Lukas. We are down to one golden wish. If Skytalker doesn't exist, how are we going to ever get out of here? How is the world ever going to change? How will the End Times ever end? How can we stop entropy from destroying everything? We are STUCK!" she wailed.

Wayan, Karma, and Hiromoto hearing the commotion all came in close.

"So, you failed Lukas?" asked Hiromoto with a superior sneer.

"No Hiromoto, I did not fail. If I had failed, do you think I would be back here? I am a man of my word."

"Lukas, please tell us what you discovered," implored Wayan as his fingers flew around the prayer beads.

"Because I don't know how to talk about what I discovered, unless we are all at the same vibrational level, I need to ask you to do something first," said Lukas.

Lukas felt like he was an orchestra conductor now with all the gang and Anna lined up in front of him as he unzipped himself on the side and took out the crystal singing bowl and the wooden baton. He left himself open and vulnerable, so all could see his insides that said sky, blue sky.

"Ok, first I need you all to just get comfortable and close your eyes. I am going to play this bowl for you and want you to concentrate on these numbers 1800422. When I am finished please remain in the silence until I tell you it is okay to talk again. Then we will speak of the experience. Everyone okay with this?" asked Lukas.

All five of them nodded in unison and in agreement. Lukas settled in, in front of the crystal bowl and struck the side lightly with the wooden baton, twice. He moved the wand around the bowl clockwise. The sound began reverberating in the dark. Anna and the gang could feel the vibration on their outer skin and in their bones. They settled in and absorbed the circular sound as if they were sponges.

Lukas continued playing the bowl for about 10 minutes as everyone was deep into the revelry of the moment. He then stopped moving the wooden baton around the rim and let the sounds slip into the dark silence of the subterranean world.

The Roman hum from the airport above capped the silence as they kept eyes closed for another ten minutes. Slowly, slowly Lukas opened his eyes and saw everyone looking at him wide-eyed. He smiled back at them.

"So, I think you probably know everything now," Lukas said.

Peachie was the first to speak. "Oh Lukas, how marvelous. How could we have known? Where did you take us?"

Lukas smiled back at him and answered, "Knock. Knock, Ireland."

Next, it was Karma. "Everything is now changed. The Queen of Ireland is so beautiful. How did you find her?"

"Long story, Karma" nodded Lukas. "But yes, it does change every-thing. Did she speak to you?"

Karma nodded his head, yes.

"I wouldn't have believed it if I hadn't heard and seen this for myself. You are not Skytalker. You are the Sky! Blue Sky," said Hiromoto.

"Yes," said Lukas. "You are right, Hiromoto. Did Mary tell you so?"

"Oh, yes, Lukas. She revealed everything. Please forgive me for all my brusque manners." Hiromoto bowed deeply.

"No worries, Hiromoto. All is forgiven. The veil of ignorance has been lifted. I believe we now all know where we have been mistaken, even me. It is now up to us to make a course correction. Don't you agree?"

"Absolutely, Lukas Sky," purred Anna. "Mary explained to me that it was important to wake up the horsemen, which I did. But, over time, their mission has been obscured by humans who had ulterior motives and personal failings. Now is the time to set history straight."

Old Gianni Patmouse, hearing all the commotion came out of his cubby hole.

"What's going on here?" he asked as he rubbed the sleep from his eyes and stroked his grey beard.

"Hmmm. It's you again. Don't try to stop us now. We now know the truth."

"What truth are you talking about?" asked Gianni.

"The truth of the Four Horsemen," answered Lukas.

"Oh, that. I tried to tell you about that a few days ago, but you wouldn't listen," yawned Gianni.

"You did? It didn't sound like the truth we now know. Sounds like you were paid off by someone to come up with Fake Truth," said Lukas.

"Ha!" scoffed Gianni. "Paid off and living in a cubby hole in the Rome airport cellar. Come on, get back down to earth with your fantasies."

"Ok. Ok, Gianni. But you said the visions of the Four Horsemen were true."

"The horsemen are true, Lukas," said Gianni. "What is in question is the interpretation. Can you be sure that what you now know is the truth?"

"Gianni, the Virgin Mary, Queen of Ireland, Queen of the Universe spoke to me when I visited the Basilica at Knock in a vision. I believe her. She touched me deep inside to the part of me that just knows things without question. The part I can trust."

"Lukas, was this your first vision ever?" asked Gianni.

"Yes! And it was beautiful," Lukas answered.

"Okay, then it will be easy to corroborate," said Gianni. "If it is indeed true, it can be affirmed by two other signs. It is always important to have three signs. Your vision was one."

"Okay, Gianni. Let's ask the gang here. They just remote viewed the Basilica in Knock. Baron gave me the coordinates. Did you all receive a different interpretation when we did the sound meditation than what you knew from the book Anna read to you?"

In unison, the group replied with a resounding, "Yes!"

"Looks like that may be five signs," said Lukas triumphantly.

"Let's hear what your horsemen have to say individually," said Gianni.

"Ok, Peachie, please go first. Tell us what you saw in the vision," urged Lukas.

"Oh, Lukas. This was marvelous. First, I felt like I floated up and out of my body. Looking down on all of us, I heard a whoosh and moved at the speed of light. Flying very fast, I could see rivers, and mountains and trees below me and then went over a big body of water. Seemed like an ocean. Then again, flew over some very, very green land until I landed near a big church. Inside was a beautiful mural made from tiny tiles. The figures in the mural came to life and talked to me."

"Who were they and what did they say, Peachie?" asked Lukas.

"It was mainly Mary who spoke. She wore a golden crown and a beautiful blue robe. She introduced herself as the Queen of the Universe and talked to all of us at once. She said that our time had passed. That is, as horsemen as was written in the Book of Revelations, the time was over and done. That prophecy was for our ancestors who were the horsemen in the old prophecy. She said to look at John. He has a book in his hand but is pointing to heaven.

"Mary said that we carried the legacy to be agents of change, but now the destruction has been mostly completed at a higher vibrational level. Something about the year 2012 ushered in a new age, and there is no need to repeat history. She also said we have new options, new ways of being, new ways to effect change to clean up the old errors and usher in a new higher level of living on the earth," said Peachie.

"What Peachie says is correct," said Wayan. "Mary spoke to us all. She said that the New Jerusalem from the prophecy was already here and has been in place for a long time. However, Mary said that there is much more for us to consider. She told us to look at the mural. It has answers to old questions. She said it is now time to honor women. It is time to realize that lies have been told for centuries by power-mongers who wanted to keep women powerless. She said that we, the NEW FOUR HORSEMEN, are to usher in a time of honoring the feminine in all, women and men."

"Wow, Wayan, that is powerful," said Lukas.

Karma spoke next. "Lukas, it is a time of great balancing. John spoke to me directly. He says he is holding a book and pointing to heaven because the answers can be suggested in books, but the real soul knowledge can only come from an interior connection with heaven, with space, from the sky. We all must find that inner sky, the inner spaciousness to really know the truth that will set us free. We can connect to the inner sky through the heart by way of the outer sky. Mary repeated a couple of times that the old ways are over and done. For those who have ears to hear, take heed."

"Hiromoto, did the vision speak to you as well?" asked Lukas.

"Yes, Lukas. I now know that as a modern horseman, I am also a samurai. I am fierce and gentle at the same time. I am a hater and a lover. I am foolish, and I am wise. I am a scoundrel and the most generous person alive. I am so much more than I could have ever known.

"The man they call the Lamb is my brother, the cross is my Father, and Mary is my Mother. Above them all is the womb of all creation, infinite intelligence, giving birth to every little thing, both male and female, equally. Consciousness is feminine. It is the womb. And it is awareness which gives birth to all. Consciousness is the mother, and all forms are the sons and daughters of awareness. I am astonished," said Hiromoto as he bowed deeply once again.

"Anna, what do you want to share with us? Anything else?" asked Lukas.

"Oh, my, my. This changes everything. First, Mary pointed out to me that these guys cannot be the Old Four Horsemen. Wrong colors. Whoever heard of a peach-colored horse or one with turquoise around his neck? Well, maybe in Tibet but not in the New Testament.

"It seemed to be true when I was reading the book, but now I am not so sure. Maybe I really wanted it to be true. I was so tired of waiting. Maybe I forced the idea? Maybe that is why we got stuck? Somehow, our ignorance saved us from ourselves. Thank God. On some level, we knew we needed you, Lukas. You have brought us the space to see clearly."

"Not so fast, everyone," said Gianni Patmouse. "That is only a second sign, and really it is just corroboration through you, Lukas. You gave them the coordinates to the Basilica which just confirms the first sign you received. What you all are about to do is change the course of history and you only have two confirmations. I would feel much better if an independent sign came forth, like one from a different book, church or painting. Or from somewhere other than the Basilica in Knock. Then and only then, will I join you to rewrite history."

Lukas looked around not sure where another sign could come from. They were still all in that dark, dank, smelly cellar of the Rome airport with the busy hum up above. What kind of sign could appear here? Wasn't it enough that the Queen of the Universe spoke to him directly and now to the horsemen suitcases and Anna? Why do we have to wait again? Wait for another sign. Lukas was sure of himself, but Gianni had sewn a seed of doubt. So, Lukas waited... again. Thank God, he had suitcase nature. It helped to master the waiting.

28

GIANNI PATMOUSE

"Lukas, Peachie, guys, let me explain a few things about this revelation," said Gianni Patmouse.

"My ancestor moved to Greece on a little island called Patmos because the world was crazy. Romans were hell-bent on grabbing and holding onto power all over the then-civilized world which stretched from England to Egypt and the Middle East, all around the Mediterranean. The Romans even destroyed the temple in Jerusalem when they felt it was time the Jews were about to revolt. I think that was about the year 70 AD."

"Christians everywhere were scared to death. They prepared themselves to die as martyrs instead of renouncing what they felt was the authentic living Christ, pure spirituality in their hearts. The first century Church was not yet organized as it is today. No one can say they were one big happy family all believing the same things. Wasn't like that. Never was. Still isn't. They did not even call themselves Christians in the first century. That came later. The first-century talk involved a lot of discussion about Jews and everybody else, Gentiles.

"A lot of these early adopters of Christianity still considered themselves Jews who had found the Messiah as had been prophesied in their books of old. My ancestor was this kind of Jew. He found it quite disturbing that a lot of Gentiles were joining the ranks considering themselves to be a part of God's chosen people, the Israelites when they didn't have lineage, blood or customs like the rest of his people. They were akin to modern-day immigrants from Africa saying they are Greek or Italian. Just not the same as the native born folks.

"It was all that damn Paul's fault. Who did he think he was taking over a leadership role in the fledgling movement? Paul of Tarsus merely had a vision that knocked him off his horse. He never even met Jesus in the flesh, and yet a lot of the modern-day Church is built around the philosophy of Paul, not that of Jesus Christ and the Apostles. Check it out.

"And there is the rub! My ancestor was truly a visionary. His revelation was filled with man's greatest fears at the time... beasts, cosmic wars, annihilation. And if you think about it, these same fears exist now.

"My ancestor, like Paul, also never actually met Christ in person. Looking at it all with the gift of hindsight combined with foresight, I realize that his visions were seen through a filter of what was going on in the world during his time, the Roman world. Are you following me so far?"

They all nodded their heads yes, in unison. Anna was off looking for pizza.

"Are you coming clean with us, Gianni?" asked Lukas.

Gianni slowly dropped his chin to his chest and then nodded his head, yes.

"You see," Gianni continued, "the visions did happen on Patmos and when my ancestor wrote them down, he searched for words to make it, let's say, a little more dramatic than it was. There were a lot of prophets around in those days. The competition was stiff. He searched back in some of the Old Testament books and copied their style, the Book of Daniel was a great find for him. He figured if it worked for Daniel, it could also work for him. You know, stay within the genre, as they say.

"But that is not the most critical part. My ancestor knew if he didn't end on a positive note, his prophecy would go the way of so many others, significant for a while, then forgotten. In this aspect, he was absolutely brilliant. He ended what is called Revelations on what is perhaps the greatest hope of people of all times, a thousand years of peace.

"Strange as it may seem, hope keeps horrible fears alive just as the horrible fears keep hope alive. This is duality, baby. Without the fears, there ain't no need for hope or even faith. A perfect hand in glove prophecy, it became quite famous. Perhaps the most famous of all times. Right up there with Nostradamus but older.

"My ancestor's vision was actually rooted in the Roman world, Roman times, Roman leadership. He couldn't openly expose that truth because the Romans would have hunted him down. Gladiators were real, crucifixions happened all the time, sending Christians to the lions was entertainment, even if you considered yourself a Jew, you were at risk.

"Appearances were everything. Still are. There was no way my ancestor was going to openly criticize the Roman world, but everyone knew that he was talking about Rome. It was an open secret.

"As a visionary and a writer, my ancestor also knew he had no control over how people would interpret his writings. No writer does. We all have our filters. However, my ancestor also had no idea how many people would misinterpret and use his words to their own ends.

"First of all, he wrote under a pseudonym. It was safer that way since this Apocalypse was so widely read. Using a pseudonym was commonplace in the day, and it allowed him freedom. Even though he never claimed it directly, he never refuted the idea that his prophecy was written by John the Apostle who also lived on Patmos and wrote the Gospel accepted in the main canon which later became the Bible.

"For quite some time, my ancestor really enjoyed the fact that his words were ascribed to John of Zebedee, the apostle, but it never was true. Later bishops and church scholars picked that up, I think Tertullian was the first to publicly contest the authorship of the Revelations piece. My ancestor's command of Greek was not as elegant as that of John who did write the fourth Gospel. My ancestor even spelled

Jerusalem differently than John did. But it took a while for anyone to analyze and question it. Fear has a way of hiding the truth. And not too many were literate in those days either. Those who could read and write remained quite busy. It was a perfect revelation that fit exactly into the times.

"The part I most regret as his relative is something no one foresaw. My ancestor was used by the powers that be to extend their abusive control. This control has been used by people like them for more than 2000 years."

"What are you talking about?" demanded Lukas, knowing that a lot was being held in the balance with his future plans.

Again, Gianni Patmouse lowered his chin and his eyes. Slowly, he looked up at the suitcases. He shook his head as he silently mouthed the words, "I am so sorry."

29

MANIPULATION UNCOVERED

"What are you sorry about, Gianni?" asked Lukas a bit impatiently.

"My ancestor published other visions, secret ones that were available to first and second century Christians. A lot of the prophets did. It was how the truth survived back then. Early Christians had mysterious symbols, secret societies, hidden meetings. It was way too risky to do things in public.

"But when Roman Emperor Constantine had his own visionary experience and converted to Christianity, it became a double-edged sword. Constantine outlawed the persecution of Christians which was a good thing while at the same time, he hijacked the whole Christian movement and he Romanized it."

"Sorry, Gianni," said Wayan, "I am not accustomed to asking for directness, but you need to be blunt with us. We have a lot riding on the line here. Our identities, our mission as Horsemen is tied up in the things written about in the Apocalypse. What do you mean that Constantine Romanized the Christian movement? And what does that have to do with your ancestor's vision?"

"Let's put it this way, folks. Everyone who is in power knows it is easy to control people who are scared. Like I said earlier, if you also give scared people hope, it is a perfect power storm. All manipulators know this. The basic formula is to scare the people, then give them hope in a direction that you supposedly control. It has worked extremely well with my ancestor's prophecy for a long, long time. Can't you see?

"In 325, at the Council of Nicaea, in what is now Turkey, a huge discussion ensued as to what to include in the Holy Bible. Roman Emperor Constantine opened the talks, but the Pope did not even attend the council. Isn't that weird? Pope Sylvester 1, sent two delegates to what has historically become one of the most critical turning points of the early church. It was this council which established the Bible and the Nicene Creed.

"Many of the discussions of what to include in the accepted teachings were readily agreed upon. However, the Book of Revelations was hotly debated. Arguments against inclusion said that it resembled more the Old Testament, not the New. Jesus didn't even seem like the same Christ as the one we know and love in the Gospels. The use of the Greek language was not elegant like the Gospel of John which led people to wonder who actually wrote Revelations.

"However, the politically savvy in the group, astute with the wielding of power, saw the advantage to including it. The powers that be at the Council of Nicaea were formulating the structure of the new church in Rome and needed a solid base. They even structured the levels of cardinals and archbishops and bishops and priests after Emperor Constantine's government structure. People don't study history, so they don't know about this. It is mostly forgotten.

"No longer was the book of Revelations interpreted to be about Ancient Rome. Now, instead, Rome became a protagonist on the side of Christ with Emperor Constantine even adopting symbols showing the defeat of the fearful dragon beast on Roman flags. Interpretations shifted to place the events outlined in Revelations to some mysterious future time to take full advantage of the fear of the unknown.

"Martin Luther, many, many years later complained about the incongruencies in the Book of Revelations but then realized it could also help his cause as he was pointing out corruption in the Church of Rome. So, he backed off and used the images of the Apocalypse to color the then current Church leadership as the beast. It worked for a short time and then backfired as that leadership turned the interpretations around to attack Martin Luther.

"So, you see, this writing has been used successfully by many for political ends over many, many years. And it still is. I really don't get why humanity is so scared of everything. Some days I wish my ancestor had never written it. It is a heavy legacy that I bear now.

"The real John of Zebedee, the original apostle of Jesus Christ, did write an Apocryphon. It was one of those secret first-century Christian books passed from devotee to devotee. You should read it sometime if you can get your hands on a copy. They ought to have one in the Vatican library."

Silence.

The combined attention of the suitcases had returned to the dark, dank silence of the cellar of the Rome airport with the hum above their heads as Gianni Patmouse stopped talking. Each was lost in a world of thought colored by confusion.

"Wow, Gianni," said Wayan. "So, what about us? We believed your ancestor's words; we have lived our lives here believing we knew who we were. We had a purpose. We were clear in our identities but stuck. We have been ready to go out and destroy one-third of the earth. Now we are perplexed. First, Mary telling us God is a woman and now you are telling us that Revelations is all made up. What's with this?" Wayan had never let on an ounce of doubt enter into his mind before this moment.

You could see a crack opening on his side, just beyond one of his zippers. Gianni Patmouse's new revelation and what he learned earlier from the remote viewing vision at Knock, had turned Wayan's world on its head.

30

❦

REGROUP

For the first time ever, Hiromoto appeared small. Nothing changed in his physical appearance except he now was not so shiny, he seemed a little dull. "Maybe we are just suitcases," he offered in a low voice, saying what no one wanted to say. "Before we came to this cellar, where were we? In closets or traveling the world with people, riding airplanes, buses, trains and in cars. Karma, I think you even have a story about being on the back of an oxcart. That is hardly the life of a horseman about to destroy one-third of the world. What the hell happened here?"

Karma sighed. "Yeah, there was the oxcart day when I went with the monk into town looking for the train to Mumbai. I never seemed to have a purpose until I arrived here with you, Hiromoto."

"The truth is," said Karma, "that I felt lost until Anna started reading to us from that Bible book when we first arrived. She is the one who planted the idea that we were the four horsemen. How could we have believed her? Maybe on some level I felt it was better to be a cellar-bound horseman than a lowly suitcase, especially a monk's suitcase. Monks never go anywhere exciting. What kind of future did that hold? At least as a horseman, I felt important, powerful, even if I was stuck."

"Hey, wait a minute, guys," chimed in Peachie. "Don't blame all this on Anna. She has been upfront with all of us from day one. She told us her story how she had been trying to get out of here for what seemed like forever. We willingly grabbed the identities of the four horsemen from that book she read to us. It gave us power. It gave us purpose when we had none. We agreed to help free her from this dismal life. It gave us energy; it gave us direction. Maybe we just took this identification thing a little too seriously. Who are we anyway? Any of us?"

Wayan shook his head, looked upward and mumbled prayers as he moved the prayer beads around his nimble fingers.

Lukas closed his eyes and listened to the hum from above.

"Who are we?" cried out Hiromoto in a deep soul-piercing scream that no one except Lukas and the other suitcases heard. The hum above was too loud. The darkness swallowed his words and his anguish.

3 1

❦

EMPTY AND FREE

"To truly realize who you are, look inside, Hiromoto," offered Lukas.

"What are you talking about?" he asked.

"First things first, Hiromoto," replied Lukas. "Open your kimono, stop being so damn belligerent. It takes vulnerability to really see, to really know, who you are. Who you are is much more than what people reflect back to you or what you read in an astrology column," continued Lukas.

"I look inside, and all I see is electronics and camera equipment, some underwear, socks, a couple of pairs of jeans and a few shirts. What can this tell me about who I am?"

"First good question, Hiromoto," winked Lukas. Karma perked up and began to listen intently to the exchange.

Lukas continued. "Empty all those things out of you. Create some space. You can no longer afford to identify with all the little things you thought were you. Most of them were given to you by someone else. You are much bigger than that," said Lukas.

Hiromoto wanted to snap at Lukas, but somehow, he felt the quiet confidence in Lukas' voice. So, he began unloading everything from the inside out. The slim camera was the last piece to go. The camera was a little difficult for Hiromoto as he was quite attached to it. In the end, he kissed it goodbye and sat in front of Lukas, open, vulnerable and full of space.

"Ok, Hiromoto," said Lukas, "please listen carefully. Take a deep breath in and release it slowly. Close your eyes and focus on your body, focus on your wheels. Really feel the connection of your wheels with the floor, the earth. Connect with every zipper and pocket, feel your handle.

"If any stray thoughts come, it is okay. In fact, it is beneficial to realize that you are aware of these thoughts. Just let them flow on like clouds in the sky on a summer day. Keep your eyes closed and focus on your physicality.

"Keep breathing," whispered Lukas, "and connect with how still you are. Really get in touch with the quality of stillness. Stay with it. Breathe deeply."

"Now, begin to connect with the silence. Not just any silence but the silence of your own voice. Hear and feel how quiet it is when your own voice is still. Outer noises may be present. That is okay. Just connect with the inner silence that begins with your own voice and opens the door to connect with the silence of your own thoughts. If a stray thought enters in, fine. Be grateful for it. It is showing you that you are aware. Just reconnect to the silence of your voice and the stillness of your body."

Lukas was enjoying the meditation as well. This was the first time he ever guided anyone except himself, and he felt it helped him go much deeper even though he stopped to talk and lead. Maybe it is a group energy thing when two or more are gathered.

"Okay, Hiromoto," said Lukas, "you have opened two doors into an inner sanctuary. Now we will open the third door. Please put your attention on your heart and connect with the spaciousness there. The whole universe is alive in your heart. Connect with the infinite space there."

At that moment, Lukas took off and felt like he was flying in vast space. Like a magic carpet ride, he was flying over a large body of water, then fields, hills, and mountains. Exhilarating! The sun shining upon him warming his body, he flowed with exhilaration, enjoying the moment when suddenly Baron came into his visionary field.

Baron, what are you doing here? Lukas asked in his mind.

"*Didn't you hear me, Lukas? I called you earlier,*" answered Baron.

What do you mean, called me? I don't have a phone, said Lukas.

"*No, not that kind of call. I sent my coordinates to you. I really need to see you. Godfrey and I have uncovered some fascinating information from the Vatican Library. Can you get up to the Sorelli's we left you at the other day?*"

Hmmm, I think I can. I will ask Peachie to help me. When do you want to meet? asked Lukas.

"*How about today at 4 pm?*" answered Baron.

Okay, see you later.

At that, Lukas' awareness flew back into his suitcase body in the cellar of the Rome airport. Completely still, he opened his eyes and noted that not only had Hiromoto participated in the meditation but also Karma, Wayan, Peachie, and even Anna. All their contents were on the floor in front of them. Enormously relaxed smiles lit up their faces.

"Okay, everyone. Please take a deep breath," said Lukas slowly and gently, "roll your wheels a little bit back and forth. Come back to this waking reality. When you are ready, please open your eyes."

Somehow, they all appeared softer and more vibrant. Hiromoto even smiled at Lukas and said, "Wow."

"Even if you want to put things back inside, I suggest that you remain empty," quietly instructed Lukas. "Forget about the contents you took out of you. Forget about them. They are like old memories, old resentments, old ideas of who you thought you were. They keep you stuck to old patterns, old ways of being. You are now free to fly in this present holy moment. I have brought you the space element. What I just showed you is the key to an incredible future. And it is all alive right here, right now. With a little practice, you will all be able to fly. So just go take it easy, relax. We can talk later," said Lukas.

"Peachie, can you come here for a minute. I need your help," said Lukas. "I have to get up to the Sorelli's where you found me last. Can you help me?"

"Sure, Lukas. What's going on?" asked Peachie.

"I am not sure but when I was in the meditation, that little boy I traveled with, Baron, came to me in a vision and said he wanted to meet me at 4 pm. Can we do it?"

"Well, it is a little early for pizza, but I think we can," said Peachie.

"Ok, thanks. By the way, how was the meditation for you?" asked Lukas.

"Wow, Lukas, it was powerful. I felt like I was flying."

"You too, eh?"

"This was amazing," said Peachie. "I want to do this again. Can you lead us again?"

"Sure, Peachie. First, though, let's meet with Baron. He has been to the Vatican Library and has some info for me. It could be the third sign we are looking for."

"Lukas, I don't think I need a third sign. When I visited the Queen of the Universe when you played the crystal bowl, I found out all I need to know. I know deep inside that it was real. I know the true meaning of the Apocalypse. The feminine is about to move into her rightful place to balance the universe. And I am going to help her do it, peacefully. She has been waiting a long time."

"I know, Peachie. I feel it too. But it is always good to have three signs. We don't want to make any careless mistakes. This is way too important. The fate of the world, our world at least, is in the balance."

"Yeah, I know. I feel like we were born for this," said Peachie.

"Yeah. I know what you mean," agreed Lukas. "The time has come."

32

BARON AND GODFREY

At a table near Sorelli's kitchen in the arrivals area of the Rome airport, Godfrey sipped an espresso macchiato, the creamy milk cooled the hot cup a little. Baron stared at the sea of people moving by. Counting them, he also began coding them by the color of their suitcases, mostly black and blue with occasional reds, oranges, and greens. He liked to count lots of different things. Numbers were important. A slight upturn at the corner of his mouth signaled the arrival of Lukas. A silent conversation ensued as Godfrey and Peachie listened in.

Hi Baron, Godfrey. Please meet Peachie, said Lukas silently.

"Nice to see you, Lukas," thought Baron. *"Hi Peachie. We don't have much time; my mother is hosting an important dinner in Parioli tonight for the Rome film festival. My tuxedo is being prepared for me now."*

Baron, you are in a pretty impressive family. Isn't Parioli near Borghese Gardens?

"Well, yes. What is more relevant, though, because of my mother I have access to the Vatican Library," said Baron.

Wow, how's that? I thought only scholars could get in there, said Lukas.

"One of mom's ancestors was a librarian at the Vatican when they first opened eons ago. He wrote a couple of books at the time. One was the first

bound cookbook about the pleasure of good food, and another was about the lives of the Popes.

"In those days, access was a privilege, and the power associated with high-level contact could be passed down by inheritance through the family. It is what made families so important here and all over Europe. Bartolomeo had a key to the library that has been passed down through the generations on the feminine side of the family. My mom has it now.

"Godfrey explained to her that I wanted to go to the Vatican library and so she gave us the key."

Baron, you are one interesting dude, said Lukas in thought.

Baron continued. *"We found a large leather-bound book called Nag Hammadi Library in English. It is named after a little town in Northern Egypt and contains secret books passed around by first-century Christians.*

"Camel driver Ali al-Samman Muhammad Khalifah was digging in the desert near Nag Hammadi for fertilizer with his friends when he found a six-foot-tall earthen jar. Next to the jar was a skeleton.

"At first, Mohammad and his companions didn't want to open the jar for fear of letting loose a djinn, you know an evil spirit, that could be guarding the antiquities but then the thought that there could be gold inside got the best of them, and they broke open the jar. Pieces of what looked like gold dust flew out. Thrilled, they danced and jumped for joy until they realized the jars were only filled with leather-bound books and the dust was from papyrus leaves. Disappointed, they gifted Mohammad the entire cache.

"He brought the books home and dumped them on the patio at his house. His mother, thinking it was trash, even used a few pages to light the fire for dinner. Soon, experts from the famous Coptic Museum in Egypt got word of the find, and the documents made their way to the museum where they have been studied intensely ever since. It was 1945.

"The more famous Dead Sea Scrolls that contained all the books of the Jewish Bible commonly known as the Old Testament in Christianity had not yet been discovered in Qumran. That happened a year or two later and became quite famous and left the Nag Hammadi find in the shadows of time.

"However, the information in the Nag Hammadi library rocked the

Christian scholarly world at the time, but little information about the find made its way into the secular world. Religious scholars could not believe what they were reading – Gospels from Apostles Thomas, Phillip, Peter, and secret works from John and others that contained the exact sayings of Jesus. Most enlightening was the Gospel of Mary Magdalene showing her as an advanced disciple of Christ and spiritual leader in first century Christendom, not a prostitute.

"The scholars took their time with their studies as these first-century writings had the power to shake the bedrock of commonly held beliefs in the Christian world. Many scholarly reputations built upon old, accepted information and dogmas could be trashed with easy acceptance of the veracity of this new find.

"Translating the books, it became obvious that the early Church had struggled with difficult questions as to what to include in the accepted doctrine. Many of the so-called heretical texts had been completely destroyed and were only known by the writings of those who warned believers against reading anything on the "not approved" list.

"Now, here in Nag Hammadi, appeared a treasure trove of the so-called heretical texts. And some of them had the same exact sayings as the New Testament of the Bible while others revealed sayings and ideas never found in the accepted canons of the Christian church. New questions arose as to what Christians actually believe about God, about Jesus Christ, about the role of women in the church.

"It wasn't until the 1970s that the first English translation appeared in circulation. So, you can see that this is really a slow-moving river of knowledge coming to light with the type of information that has a long history and far-flung future implications."

So, what does that have to do with me? asked Lukas. Early Christianity overflowed with prophets who claimed first-hand knowledge and contact with God. Gianni Patmouse has made that abundantly clear to all of us. Lots of competition existed among the visionaries of the time.

"You don't understand, Lukas," thought Baron. "In those days, the important knowledge was passed around in secret books, not public visions and decrees. It was too risky to be open about those things as Christ had already

been crucified as well as lots of the other early Christians including the apostle Peter and Jesus' brother James, to keep their radical ideas in check.

"These secret sacred texts point to so many important truths such as the feminine aspect of God which is the source of everything here on earth. The Vatican Library, and not even in the Secret Archives, contains it all in plain sight, continued Baron. It is an open secret' that I imagine you can also find on the shelves of Barnes and Noble and on Amazon.

There are lots of things in the Vatican Library, Baron. Isn't it still considered heresy to question the accepted doctrine? asked Lukas.

"Exactly right, Lukas. And that is one of the main points. Who decided what was heresy and what was orthodox? Were they right? How do we know? Besides, it was the Apostle, "Doubting Thomas" who wrote the Gospel of Thomas that has recorded the 'living words' of Jesus Christ. Was he also a heretic? He was an Apostle."

Wow, Baron, you are talking a lot, silently that is, said Lukas.

"I really have something important to say."

Baron, do you remember when we were in Ireland? The mural spoke to me. Mary told me through thought transference that the feminine is the mother of all. Joseph was kneeling in prayer and John was pointing to heaven but, Mary was holding the energy of creation in between her hands in front of her heart. The Creator is feminine. God, the Creator, is a woman, said Lukas.

"I know. I heard Mary too," said Baron.

Why didn't you tell me? asked Lukas.

"You know I don't like to use a lot of words, Lukas. But it was her words that got me thinking about going to the Vatican Library. The Apostle John is holding a book but pointing to heaven. What could it all mean? They were silent like I am. So, it was up to us to figure it out. They liked to use riddles and say things like 'For those with ears to hear.'"

Ok, ok. So, what does all this mean now? asked Lukas.

"I met an American lady scholar in the library named Elaine. She was talking about a lot of things regarding early Christians. She said that Revelations, as portrayed in the Bible, is highly contested, very political. Always has been a lot of politics going on with the Vatican. Did you know it is also a country in addition to being the head of the Catholic Church?

Lukas nodded yes.

"Francis, the current Pope, and all-around good guy has been shaking up some of the old structures."

Yeah, I realize that, said Lukas. I heard that he lives in constant danger of assassination. One time in the distant past, the Popes even left Rome and allied themselves with the King of France because there was so much political intrigue. They lived in France for a long time before returning to Rome.

"Yes. That is part of the political nature of the Vatican," said Baron.

Hmmm, thought Lukas, Gianni Patmouse said the same thing about Revelations and the Apocalypse being a politically motivated document. Something is going on here.

In John's Secret Book, he had a vision where God says, 'I am the Father, I am the Mother, I am the Son.' Why was this hidden? What is wrong with God being a woman too?"

Can you repeat that, Baron? asked Lukas.

"Lukas, God's first thought was the feminine version of himself, and it is she, herself, who is the Mother of everything."

Wow, Baron. The suitcase gang downstairs taught me that thoughts are things and that thoughts create. I am going to have to sit with this a bit. It's a big change of direction for me.

You are saying God is a woman and she created the world? Why is this not even hinted at in the Bible? asked Lukas.

"Good question. Obviously, the people in power in the early times of Christianity and at the Council of Nicaea did not agree with this version of reality.

"If you read the history, first century Christianity had lots of women followers and leaders. By the time the third century rolled around, it was all men at the Council of Nicaea. Did you know that Peter was very jealous of Mary Magdalene and her closeness with Jesus?"

How do you know this about Peter? asked Lukas. Wasn't he the first Pope?

"Some scholars say Mary Magdalene should have been the first Pope. She was that powerful of a leader. She kept the Apostles calm after the crucifixion of Jesus. You can imagine how frightened they must have been. Even Peter denied his association with Christ three times "before the cock crowed". It was

Mary Magdalene who reminded them of their holy mission and urged them to put on the "Perfect Man" as they liked to call their higher self. She took the leadership role and held them together."

Wow, Baron. This is a lot to swallow, said Lukas.

"Enough for now. All you need to know is the four horsemen are a modern-day fiction. It is an outer prophecy used by power mongers across time to scare the masses to keep them in line. The real change, the real evolution, the real apocalypse is interior, secret and sacred, nothing to be afraid of. It is for those who have ears to hear and eyes to see. The feminine is poised to birth this knowledge into the world, and the modern horsemen are here to help her spread the word. Perhaps that will feel like the end times to the old power structures. It probably should."

Baron, I hate to bring this up at this moment. But how do we know this new info isn't just from a competing group of prophets? Or perhaps it was mistranslated?

"Lukas, the only way you can know anything is to settle deep inside yourself. Be quiet and listen to that still, small voice. That voice brings us to a space of deep inner knowing. It is the one you can trust, not the outer intellect.

"In the end, this is the whole point to everything. None of us need an intermediary between God and us. There is a direct line for those willing to go inside and make contact. God lives in that still, small space in our hearts, sees all, hears all and can read the truth of our innermost selves."

"Excuse me, Baron," Godfrey chimed in, "We have to go now. Your mother's dinner is beginning soon. Please say goodbye to your friends."

Godfrey stood up, ran his hand through his thick sandy blonde greying hair and began walking for the door. Baron followed, looking straight ahead, appearing to all the world like his mind was vacant. But we all know better.

"Bye, Lukas, Bye Peachie," Baron said silently in his mind

Bye, Baron.

33

RIGHT QUESTIONS

"Peachie, why didn't you ever tell me I could get up to the arrivals terminal by way of Sorellis?" asked Lukas.

"You never asked that question, Lukas. You only ever wanted to go to Departures for Cancun. Remember only right questions elicit right answers," said Peachie.

"Hoo boy," said Lukas, "this is beginning to feel like another secret in plain sight. We could have always left the basement if we went through arrivals and not departures. My, my, my we have to think backward to move forward now."

"I hope Anna and the boys will believe us when we tell them what Baron told us," said Peachie.

"Don't worry," said Lukas, "I have a plan to let all of them experience this for themselves. Baron shared some numbers with me that will help."

34

EAST AND WEST

"Gianni, please come here."

The little grey-haired mouse strolled over to Anna and the boys.

Anna screamed. "Lukas, I do not like mice! Hiromoto, please get rid of him."

Hiromoto rolled over to obey Anna, but Lukas stopped him.

"Wait just a minute, Hiromoto," said Lukas. "I want you all to hear what Gianni has to say. Go ahead, Gianni."

"Hey everyone. I have been watching all of you for a while now. Has been entertaining. It always is when we get to observe beings who put on different identities. Why do you think we make such heroes out of movie stars? They are great, but hey, you guys were even greater. Each of you deserves an Oscar."

"What are you talking about, little mouse?" asked Hiromoto.

"I watched the four of you roll into this basement, lost, alone in the dark. Anna helped each of you by reading from my book, and you each willingly believed yourself to be a horseman. You each took on an identity that felt comfortable to you like you were putting on a new suit. It was all so plausible, after all, we are in Rome and like they say, when in Rome do as the Romans. But the big news is that none of it is true. Hell, they even made-up hell. The powers that be made it all up to keep the masses in line. Fear is a great motivator.

"My ancestor, the author of Revelations with the pseudonym, John from Patmos had his vision embellished upon and spun over the ages by men in power in order to scare and give hope in the same moment. A powerful combination – hope and fear - but it all... the apocalypse, revelations, everything... already happened, in ancient Rome. It was all fulfilled during the time of Nero. I wish there were residuals for this story as it goes on and on, but there are not. It is all public domain. I am coming clean. It is time the world knew this and gave up its fear habit."

"You are just confirming what Mary, the Queen of Ireland told us in that last vision we jointly had," said Karma. "Lukas, I think we have the third sign."

"Yeah, I think we do, Karma," agreed Lukas, "but let's take this a step further. It's important. I have the crystal bowl here and some coordinates for the Vatican Library. Now that you all know how to meditate, and remote view let's take a sound journey to the library and confirm our last bit of information from Baron."

"What's that info, Lukas?" asked Wayan.

"Baron told us he found an important book in the Vatican Library that confirms early Christians knew that God was feminine and masculine. He surmises a grand political power struggle took place during the first, second and third centuries blotting out ideas and hiding the feminine power of God. This is reflected in modern-day societies as well. Most of the holy books have carried this interpretation bias against the feminine ever since."

"In the East, we always have revered women," said Wayan. "We know there are feminine deities. Seems only the Christians, Jews, and Muslims have this problem. Look at what that has caused in the world!"

" You may be right, Wayan, said Lukas, "but look at your cultures in the East. Women are not any better off than in the West. Women have been plastered and put down all over the world. Women are subject to such humiliation at the hands of men, it should be considered a crime instead of normal. But women are waking up. It is time for men and women to walk together equally in this world. It is time that we all recognize the importance of the feminine power inside each of us whether we are men or women. But more than recognize it, it is time to honor it and bring it to the forefront."

Karma chimed in, "Ever hear of Tara? She is a full-fledged Buddha. When the other enlightened beings realized there was a "new light" illuminated in the world, they began a search for the enlightened person. They were shocked to find a woman. So, they told her 'Now that you are enlightened, a Buddha, you can reincarnate as a man.' At this Tara answered, 'I will always be born as a woman!'

"We are not perfect," answered Wayan.

"I remember hearing that Buddhist nuns were considered inferior because they had forgotten some of their vows," said Peachie. "Buddhist monks have 227 vows while nuns have 337. Just doesn't make sense to my Western mind."

"Maybe the whole world needs to reflect on the feminine and take action to change to honor women," said Karma.

"Maybe, you are right, Karma," agreed Lukas. "And it has nothing to do with women overpowering men. It has everything to do with women stepping into their true feminine power and walking alongside men together in this world, equals in all ways and yet respecting differences. In this way the Divine Feminine and the Divine Masculine can become one."

"What do you all think?" asked Lukas. "Want to remote view the library? Maybe it will give us greater insight into solving this dilemma."

"Let's do it," they chimed simultaneously.

35

0669879411

"Gianni, please join us," said Lukas. "Everyone, please get comfortable."

Lukas unzipped his side and pulled out a crystal singing bowl. Wayan pulled a small bell out of his front pocket, Karma found an old bucket that he turned upside down to use as a drum. Hiromoto had an over-sized peppercorn grinder from Sorellis for percussion.

Lukas began by striking the crystal bowl a couple of times and then moved the baton around the edge in a clockwise direction. Like an ethereal jazz quintet, each of the suitcases joined in. Anna began to tone vocally, and Gianni kept the beat with his clapping hands and tapping feet. Otherworldly sounds slipped from this unlikely magical group around the corners into the darkness and surrounded them like a cocoon.

One by one, Lukas enunciated numbers Baron had given him. Zero, six, six, nine, eight, seven, nine, four, one, one. Zero, six, six, nine, eight, seven, nine, four, one, one. Zero, six, six, nine, eight, seven, nine, four, one, one.

Together the group stopped their playing and entered into the stillness, silence, and spaciousness of a deep remote viewing meditation. Lukas kept rounding the crystal bowl with his baton, slowly. They arrived at the Vatican Library almost simultaneously, floating invisibly above the old books near the domed blue ceiling painted with angels, lace, and tiny white flowers. In another moment, the leather-bound Nag Hammadi book floated up to them and scenes from the book came to life. A host of characters from the first century of the modern age formed a circle as if in a theater in the round. Lukas and his group had floating front row seats.

The pages of the over-sized book turned themselves. And a male character in a beige robe the color of desert sand common to the time of the first century Middle East stepped to the center, pointed to the woman dressed in blue, and said, "Mary, you must leave our group for women are not deserving of life."

Jesus stepped forward, in front of Mary as if to protect her and said, "Simon Peter, take back your words. I, myself shall teach Mary so that she may become a living spirit resembling you men. For every woman who will make herself a living spirit will enter the Kingdom of Heaven."

Mary, with pieces of her long brown hair slipping out the side of a blue veil, moved to the center with Jesus. She smiled and cried at the same moment as Simon Peter moved off center stage and into the group around the edge.

Mary asked Jesus, "Will everything be destroyed or not?"

The Savior answered, "All forms will be dissolved into their own roots. The nature of the elements is resolved into the root of its nature alone. He who has ears to hear."

Jesus then moved off center stage and into the background. Mary stayed center stage, it seemed as if time had passed and she appeared to have been crying. Peter came forward, stood above her as she was seated on a rock. He said, "Sister Mary, we know that Jesus, our Lord and Savior loved you more than the rest of women. Please share with us the things he told you in private."

Mary Magdalene shared the secrets of her heart with the group of apostles as they all came in close to hear her gentle and wise voice. She ended with this teaching.

"Time is an illusion. All things are happening now. There is no past, there is no future. There is no past memory, there is no legacy. It is all recall. Remembering something into the now, right now, is a new creation. We creator beings, sons and daughters, in the image of God the Father and God the Mother, continually create the right now. This is the open secret of the ages, for those who have ears to hear."

Peter abruptly moved to center stage. In a loud commanding voice, he said, "I, for one, do not believe the Savior said this. These teachings are extremely bizarre. Are we going to forget what we know and listen to her? Did Jesus really prefer her to us?"

Mary wept and said, "Dear brother Peter, what do you think? Do you think I made all this up myself, or that I am lying about the Savior?"

Levi stepped forward and said to Peter, "Peter you have always been hot-tempered. Now I see you are fighting with our beloved Mary like you fight with the adversaries. If our Lord and Savior made her worthy, as he told us he would, who are you to reject her? Surely Jesus knows her very well. That is why he loved her more than us."

"Instead," continued Levi, "we should be ashamed of ourselves and put on the cloak of the "Perfect Man" as our Lord taught us. In this way, we can make personal contact with Him as he commanded us to do. Remember, we are to preach the good news of the gospel and not lay down any other law or rule beyond what our Savior told us."

Peter walked out of the center of the circle into the darkness of one of the corners of the library brooding.

First century Christians joyfully filled the atmosphere as the secret books revealed more and more with living words that penetrated each of the suitcase's souls as well as that of Gianni Patmouse.

Christ arrived in a golden mist with Mother God and Father God on each side of him. Without a word, he smiled at each of the suitcases and made the sign of the cross. Each one of them, Anna, Hiromoto, Karma, Wayan, Peachie, Lukas and even Gianni, became intimately aware of the timeless truth deep inside. They seemed to sparkle with bright light as they floated.

Thunder shook the building as the three – Father, Son and Mother

- formed one combined image of sparkling light. A silent voice entered the spaciousness of each heart present and revealed:

"I am, always was and always will be. I am male and female. I am neither male nor female. I am you and you are another myself. Look into your own heart and you will see. Look into your own mind and you will hear. I AM, AUM, I AM THAT I AM, OM. Be still and know that I AM God."

With complete certainty, they all knew they really were so much more than suitcases. They were set free from their limited identities, their limited beliefs. The Truth was now known. Love and peace surrounding them were palpable. Their auras blazed brightly as beautiful, joyous laughter, like tinkling bells filled the air.

Lukas stopped the rounds on the bowl bringing the group gently back to the underground world at the Rome airport. Sitting in silence, a knowing smile took over the entire group mind. Time floated. Gnosis enveloped everyone. The visions faded with the sounds into the invisible realms. And each of them sat in bliss, forever changed by that holy moment.

After a long while, Lukas gently chimed in, "Feel your connection with the floor. Move your zippers slowly. Come back to this reality of the Rome airport cellar and gently open your eyes."

Gianni Patmouse was the first to speak. "Wow, man. I ain't never smoking pot again. Tell me where I can get one of those crystal bowls, Lukas."

36

GUADALUPE

"Lukaaas! Lukaaas!"

"Baron? Is that you?" called Lukas.

Lukas heard his name being called again. It seemed to be coming from above in the air conditioning ducts. It was Baron, calling him out loud!

Lukas moved to the nearest duct. "Baron, can you hear me?" asked Lukas.

"Yes, Lukas. Listen. I know you used the coordinates and went to the library. What do you and the gang think about all of this?"

"Wow, Baron. This changes everything."

"It sure does, blue boy!" said Baron.

"Blue Boy, ha-ha. Is that my new nickname?" asked Lukas.

"I can give you a number or call you Blue Sky Boy if you prefer," said Baron.

"No, that's okay. Blue Boy is good with me," said Lukas.

"Listen, my mother wants to go to Mexico City to visit the Virgin of Guadalupe shrine. And guess what. We are stopping in Cancun on the way. Want to go?"

"Are you kidding? I have been waiting an eternity to get back to Cancun. When do you leave?"

"We are checking in soon. Get up here. Godfrey and I will wait at Sorelli's for you."

"Ooookaaaay! Be right there. Just going to say goodbye to the guys and Anna."

"Hey, Anna, Hiromoto, Karma, Wayan and Peachie please come here," said Lukas.

Lukas heard distinct wheels rolling on concrete in the dark, coming closer to him as he was zipping up the crystal bowl inside of himself.

"Hey there. I want to say goodbye. My ticket back to Cancun has arrived. My flight is leaving soon."

"Awww, Lukas," said Peachie, "I, for one, will miss you intensely. You are the cutest damn suitcase I have ever met." He kissed Lukas on the cheek and gave him a squeeze.

"Peachie, if you ever make it to Cancun, let me know. I will make sure you get a ride from the airport to my house."

"Thanks, Lukas," smiled Peachie.

"Blessings, Lukas," said Wayan. "May the longtime sun shine upon you wherever you may roll," he said as he fingered his prayer beads.

"Blessings to you too, Wayan. Thanks for being my friend when I really needed one," said Lukas.

"Namaste."

"Lukas, may all causes and conditions bring you fortunate outcomes," intoned Karma in what seemed like three-part harmony.

"Thanks, Karma. Stay balanced, Bud," Lukas put his hands together in prayer position and gave him a slight bow.

"Tashi Delek."

"Lukas, you opened my eyes," said Hiromoto. "You lifted the veil with your meditations and sounds. We now know we will help usher in the age of the feminine in a peaceful, balanced manner. If you ever need anything from the right-hand side of the world, just think 222.555, and I will respond. You are so much more than a suitcase. Don't forget," he said as he bowed deeply.

"Thanks, Big Guy. Glad you are on my team, or maybe I am on yours," said Lukas with a double wink.

"Shukufuku," said Hiromoto.

"Adios," said Lukas.

"So, you did it Big Boy," said Anna. "You brought us space, you liberated us from our stuckness, you showed us ancient truths. You are Skytalker. No mistakes were made," she said with a huge smile.

"Aw Anna, thank you for summoning me. Sure, life would have been less stressful if I had never missed my flight to Cancun in the first place but somehow, it was my destiny to come here to be with you and the guys. I have come to know myself as something much grander than I ever thought possible. And it is because of you."

"Lukas, I was only the instigator. You did the soul-searching; you released all that was not you to discover who you really are. You helped us all realize that our identities were so limited, and we are all so much more than we could have ever realized. And personally, for me, I am so happy that you had your meetings with Baron in the Sorelli's in arrivals. If not for that, I would never have gotten back with Big Jim."

"What do you mean, Anna? Did you find Big Jim at Sorelli's?" asked Lukas.

"Big Jim started hearing about a blue and orange suitcase hanging around Sorelli's. He knows those are my favorite colors. So, he got a job as an assistant manager. He saw you with Baron but waited for me to show to get some pizzas. Now he is going to take me home to our palace in the mountains. I am done with the underworld thanks to you. And I still have one golden wish left."

With that Anna dropped her suitcase identity and stepped out as one of the most gorgeous women Lukas had ever seen. Her turquoise dress reflected her blue, blue eyes as her smile filled the room.

"Wow, Anna. Is that what a golden wish can do?" asked Lukas.

"Lukas, through you and all the space you brought us, I was able to get myself back together again. This is who I really am. Now it is time to find Big Jim and go home."

"I am so happy for you Anna, but what about the guys?" asked Lukas.

"Oh, they are all free to leave now. I suggest that they go up to the airport and find some good humans with whom to travel. We are all unstuck. The truth has made us all free. Arrivederci, Lukas."

37

WHAT NOW?

Sofia returned home to Mexico from the retreat center. Seems like the old trauma had slipped into a distant past. Thank God. She began sifting through her mail when she found a claim form from Etruscanair.

"Wow. How do I do this? I got all my clothes and shoes back from that box sent from Ireland, but my crystal singing bowl, the little cloth bag with three gold coins and my suitcase are still missing. How do I fill out this form?"

"Buongiorno. Etruscanair. How may I help you."

"Hello, my name is Sofia O'Malley. I just received an email with a claim form for a lost suitcase. Can you help me please?"

"Of course, Madame. Please, will you provide me with the case number."

"Sure, it is FCOA219749."

"Oh yes, Ms. O'Malley. We found your suitcase, sent it to Rome and put it on Etruscan Flight A02492. Hmmm but it looks like we lost it again and never found it. Sorry. For that, we sent you a claim form."

"Excuse me, what did you say your name was?"

"Rafaele."

"Rafaele, ciao. You were the first person I talked to at the call center. This is our third time speaking!"

"Ms. O'Malley, anything is possible, especially here. How can I help you?"

"Last week, well I think it was last week, my sense of time is a bit skewed right now. So, let's just say, a couple of weeks ago, a box arrived from Ireland with my clothes and shoes in it. But my suitcase was not included nor my crystal singing bowl nor a little cloth bag with some valuables."

"That's strange, Ms. O'Malley. Etruscanair doesn't fly to Ireland. How do you think I can help?"

"What should I claim, Rafaele?"

"What have you lost?"

"Now there is a good question to ponder, Rafaele. Thank you. I will be back in touch soon."

"Arrivederci."

"Arrivederci."

38

⚬≫⚬

THE MISSED CALL

Sofia's phone showed a missed call, an unknown Cancun number.

"Buenas tardes, good afternoon. I have a missed call from this number, my name is Sofia."

"Sofia O'Malley?"

"Yes. How can I help you?" she asked.

"Have you lost a suitcase?"

"Well, yes but it has been a while. Why do you ask?"

"We found a suitcase in baggage claim today. No one picked it up, and it has your name and phone number on the tag. I am calling from the Cancun airport."

"Really? Oh wow." Sofia could not believe what she was hearing after all this time.

"Can you please describe your lost suitcase?" asked the baggage claim official.

"Well, yes. It is a beautiful blue suitcase with a handsome orange stripe on the top front. If you open it up, inside you will see the light blue silky material with the words blue sky imprinted in the material and a metallic nameplate that says Lukas S. O'Malley. By chance have you opened the suitcase?" asked Sofia.

"No ma'am, we have not. We can though."

"Please do."

"There is nothing inside except a crystal singing bowl, a baton and a little cloth bag."

"That's it! That's my suitcase!" screamed Sofia.

39

CANCUN

"Can you believe it? They found Lukas! And in Cancun! Feels like the final pieces of a jigsaw puzzle coming together, Fernando."

Sofia's big golden red cat looked up at her and yawned.

Quickly Sofia grabbed her purse, jumped in the car and drove to the airport. The parking lot in front of the new terminal was not yet finished. *Free parking! Lady Luck is certainly with me today!*

"I wonder if I get to collect $200 dollars as I pass GO! Feels like a super lucky day," said Sofia out loud to no one in particular.

She locked the Jetta and noticed a man with two different colored brown eyes, one light, one dark at the door of the airport as she walked in. He smiled at her and said hello as he held the door open. He had an American accent and beautiful blonde greying hair. Sofia felt like she knew him but couldn't be sure. She paused a moment and wanted to stop to talk but didn't as she saw Lukas right away. Hurrah!

"Señora, may I please see your ID? asked the luggage attendant.

"Sure," said Sofia.

"Ok, thank you, Ms. O'Malley. Here are your five suitcases."

"What? What are you talking about? I thought it was just one."

"Each one has your name and phone number on it. A peach colored one, a titanium one, a big red leather one with turquoise beads around the handle and this cloth bag with colorful Indonesian exit stamps and of course the handsome blue one with the orange stripe."

Sofia looked up and saw a little boy with bright blue eyes staring at her. He seemed magical, almost like he was floating in a sparkly aura of light illuminated by a huge smile. In her mind, Sofia heard, *just say gracías.*

The attendant helped wheel the five bags to Sofia's Jetta. She handed him $500 pesos and said, "Gracías, Señor."

Sofia was delayed leaving the parking lot as a caravan of Federal Police cars pulled up, lights flashing. A small, handcuffed man stepped out of the car and entered the gate for flights to Acapulco. Sofia took a deep breath and turned her silver Jetta south.

She thought, *So Lukas, what have you been up to? Who are your friends? You are all just in time to accompany me to Italy, not Rome but Naples. It is Italy but so different than the rest of the country. Are you ready for a new world? A new life?*

"Sofia, I love you so much! These are my friends from Rome. Actually, we met in the Rome airport, and we have some important work to do together. The world depends upon us. But before we go back to Italy, can we go to the beach? I have told them about the beautiful sand, the turquoise sea, the palm trees, cool coconut water, bikini clad women, cabana boys. Please, Sofia?"

"Lukas, have you learned to talk?" Sofia was flabbergasted at how deep his voice was.

"Siiiiiiiii! The world is not really like we think it is. There is so much more. So much beauty, so much love for those who have eyes to see and ears to hear," said Lukas out loud.

"And I thought you were just a suitcase. A damn fine suitcase but now you can talk! This world surprises me every single day! Let's go home and yes! Let's go to the beach! I want to hear all about your adventures."

<<<<>>>>

The End

40

AFTERWORD

Some time ago, I realized that most fiction contains true elements from the author's life. LOST Baggage is no different. These books began their lives because of the frustration of losing suitcase in Rome but I found with the aid of fiction, I could better express the deeper ideas, especially in the magically realistic part of the story. The pivotal choice of turning this story into a novel allowed me to speak freely about how I felt about characters, events and places that were now fictionalized and malleable.

All the names, characters, places and timeframes are fictionalized or used in a fictionalized manner except for Fernando, the cat. Any resemblance to anyone living or dead is purely coincidental. The Nag Hammadi Library in English is a real book that can be purchased on-line or in bookstores. However, I have paraphrased passages and used the information in a fictional manner. For scholarly study, I suggest you refer directly to the book.

By the way, one part of the story that is true is that I have lost luggage in Rome four times.

Notes:

Nag Hammadi Library in English, Third Revised Edition. Copyright 1988 E.J. Brill, The Netherlands. Translated by members of the Coptic Gnostic Library Project of the Institute for Antiquity and Christianity, James M. Robinson, Director.

Sections of this book have been paraphrased, namely excerpts from The Secret Apocryphon of John, pages 105, The Gospel of Thomas, p.113-114 and the Gospel of Mary p.7, 18-19. These passages form the ideas about the remote viewing scenes in the Vatican Library. My intent was to keep the essence of the meaning as I understood it but to make the information more readable. It is my personal interpretation of this scholarly work. Any error is mine alone and not done with intention to mislead but only to illuminate.

∞

❧

Marie shares her time between Italy, Mexico and the U.S.A. When she is not hiking the Himalayas, enjoying the floating markets of Bangkok or taking time to smell the flowers in Bali, she loves to garden, commune with her big golden, red cat and share intimate moments with Infinite Intelligence.

❧

∞